EBURY PRESS AND BLUE SALT
THE PHOENIX

Bilal Siddiqi is a novelist and screenwriter based in Mumbai. He is the author of *The Stardust Affair, The Kiss of Life* (co-written with actor Emraan Hashmi) and *The Bard of Blood*, a spy novel which he wrote when he was nineteen and which was adapted by Red Chillies Entertainment into a Netflix show. Siddiqi was also the creator of this show and worked on the screenplay. *The Phoenix* is his fourth book.

THE PHOENIX

BILAL SIDDIQI

BLUE SALT

EBURY
PRESS

An imprint of Penguin Random House

EBURY PRESS

USA | Canada | UK | Ireland | Australia
New Zealand | India | South Africa | China

Ebury Press is part of the Penguin Random House group of companies
whose addresses can be found at global.penguinrandomhouse.com

Published by Penguin Random House India Pvt. Ltd
7th Floor, Infinity Tower C, DLF Cyber City,
Gurgaon 122 002, Haryana, India

Penguin
Random House
India

First published in Ebury Press and Blue Salt by Penguin Random House India 2020

ISBN 9780143447771

Typeset in Sabon by Manipal Technologies Limited, Manipal
Printed at Thomson Press India Ltd, New Delhi

www.penguin.co.in

MIX
Paper
FSC FSC® C010615

Acknowledgements

This book is a work of fiction interspersed with a few realities to create a believable plot. The characters, the situations and the storyline, however, are all figments of my imagination. I wrote this book to entertain, not educate, and I hope I have succeeded at that. I have always been an ardent fan of espionage novels and films. *The Phoenix* is my second attempt at a spy thriller, after *The Bard of Blood*.

The bravery of Indian intelligence officials and defence personnel far surpasses that of characters penned down by novelists. So I'd like to thank all those involved in keeping our country safe.

S. Hussain Zaidi Sir, thank you for always standing by me and helping me realize my dream of becoming a writer. Like a true mentor and father figure, you are willing to do for me more than I would be willing to do for myself. Love to you and the family—Velly Ma'am, Zain and Ammar—always.

Thank you, Milee Ashwarya, for being extremely supportive and for offering insights and creative pointers that helped shape this book as well as my previous work. It's a delight to have a publisher like you to lean back on when the writing gets hard!

Thank you to Roshini Dadlani who has helped shape and tighten the narrative of this book. Vineet Gill has been extremely prompt and thorough in editing it. Sorry for my erratic delivery dates, and thanks for making this book happen. Thank you to Khyati Behl for all her marketing efforts. Thank you, Devangana, for this unique cover. You are truly one of the best in the business!

A big thank you to Shah Rukh Sir for the warmth and encouragement that he showers upon me. He is and always will be an inspiration to me. (Goes without saying, I'm just one of the billions he has touched and inspired.)

After *The Bard of Blood* and *The Kiss of Life*, I have found a true friend and brother in Emraan Hashmi. He is someone I can call with the smallest of worries and who, after he has had a good laugh, comes up with solutions to tackle them. Thank you for the love, Emi, Parveen and Ayaan!

My friends—Veer, Nabeel, Siddhesh—have stuck by me through thick and thin. The friends you make in school are all that you need to get by.

And finally, my family: my grandmother, Hamida; my parents, Farhat and Mansoor; and my sister, Zayna.

It may seem like I take you all for granted, but I don't. I love you all more than I can put down here. More of that in my autobiography whenever there's one.

Now to the good (hopefully) spy stuff . . .

To Pallavi Pawar, my English teacher in school.

Thank you for believing in my abilities ever since I was a kid and for instilling in me the confidence to write. I owe you a lot. Love you always, Miss P!

In order to rise
From its own ashes
A phoenix
First
Must
Burn.

—Octavia E. Butler, *Parable of the Talents*

1

2013: Southall, London

Maqsood Akram looked nothing like he used to. The pictures the Indians had of him would get them nowhere. After several surgeries, his nose was sharper and his jaw more angular than what he had been born with. Of late, he had decided never to keep a beard when he was in a country he didn't call home. The racist skinheads couldn't tell the difference between an Indian Sikh and a Talibani warrior if their mothers' lives depended on it. But they would, nonetheless, go after both.

Akram stepped out of a store after having bought himself a pack of condoms. He made a few calls to his pimp, who promised to send him the best he could later that night. Akram gave him the address of a moderately priced hotel in the vicinity. He couldn't have his followers witnessing his debauchery. Illicit sex, alcohol and even drugs: haraam of the highest order. And if they could see how easily he procured these unholy pleasures, they would have strayed from the path he had set them on with much difficulty.

He lit a cigarette as he walked through the crowded Southall market, brushing past the several Indian men and women whom he had sworn to wipe off the face of the earth when he set up his organization in the rugged terrain of north Pakistan. He had named it Azaad Jihad Fauj, which was secretly funded by the PIA, Pakistan Intelligence Agency, through multiple shell corporations. Southall, a suburban district of west London, teemed with Indians. And he hated the irony. To kill his enemies he had to first live among them.

The Indians were hot on his heels. A failed assassination attempt on him had led the PIA to transfer him out of the country and into one of their sleeper cells in an innocuous locality in Southall. From here, his handlers promised, he would be allowed to chart out his future activities. He could use the local radicalized youth recruited by them and their different underbosses to his advantage. And the Indians would have no clue.

A faint shower fell from the grey London sky. Akram, irritated, began to walk more briskly towards his neighbourhood. He took a deep final drag and threw his cigarette aside. A Gujarati shopkeeper he knew waved at him and began to walk towards him with a dog on a leash. Akram reciprocated with a smile, masking his hatred for both the shopkeeper and his dog.

'Funny thing,' the shopkeeper began when he was near enough, speaking with a British twang he had developed over the years. 'All this rain and there seems to be some issue with the plumbing in our block. No water.'

Akram shrugged. 'Nothing to be worried about though, is there?'

'A plumber has arrived,' he replied. 'Said he'll take an hour to fix it.'

'Have a good day then,' Akram said, eager to stem the conversation and reach his lodgings.

When he entered his apartment, he saw three of his men offering namaaz. There were parcels of unopened food awaiting them, with four clean plates on a dining mat.

The same old routine, Akram thought. The same damn gravies and naan from the local Pakistani eatery, which made sad versions of the rich delicacies he enjoyed back home in Bahawalpur, Punjab, in Pakistan. The same painful conversation about a beautiful afterlife with young idiots who were going to blow themselves up at some point. The same propagation of an Islam he knew not to be true. But terror was a lucrative business. And he was a good businessman who could sell religion to these young fools.

Anyway, just two hours to go, he thought to himself as he checked his wristwatch. Then he would be screwing some young girl and guzzling alcohol. There were worse ways to live. He had been to Afghanistan. To Iraq. To India. Fought wars. Killed people. He spoke proudly to his recruits of the blood he had shed in the 26/11 attacks in Mumbai. A gleaming jewel in his crown, he would always say. Too much had been done, but it wasn't over yet.

He was in the final stages of plotting a major attack on the Indian Army barracks in Kashmir. And these three fools, who had just got done with their prayers, were about to carry it out. All this while he would be nestled up in this comfortable little flat in London. And as the PIA assured him, the Indians would have no clue . . .

The Indians, however, did have a clue. More than a clue. They had picked up an interesting piece of intelligence through their network of spies in Pakistan. In their communications with Akram, the PIA had slipped up ever so slightly.

Akram's proxy network had kicked in five seconds too late when he called up his handler stationed in Islamabad. Instead of seeming to emanate from the African continent, the call transmitted its true location in west London. It was in the sixth second that London changed to Zambia, Africa. The Indian agent who was monitoring these 'secure' communications spotted the lapse and alerted his seniors. After six months of groundwork and fact-checking, Director General Amarjyot Bhushan sent four of his trusted field officers to London, despite his superiors strictly advising against it.

Amarjyot had enemies within the agency as well. The Intelligence and Research Wing, or the IRW, was India's main spy agency that operated both within the country and internationally. The bureaucratic nature of the agency never supported the maverick methods that Amarjyot stood for. Being a soldier first, Amarjyot always thought of the most effective forms of attack. Dialogue and discussions came next. But the bureaucrats did not approve of this approach. And one such officer, Bipin Sharma, was vying for Amarjyot's position, making it a point to openly disapprove of his ways.

To circumvent this red-tapism, Amarjyot had assembled a covert unit within his ranks. It included four people whom he trusted as much as himself, if not more. And trust didn't come cheap in their world. He called this group, which he too was a part of, the Phoenix 5. They all knew that their activities would usually fall outside the official purview of the IRW, and that their missions would not be sanctioned by the top brass of the intelligence community for the most part. But they would do what they needed to do for the greater good. And they had the necessary skills to pull it off.

These four were now in London, about to take Akram out, once and for all. No capture, no interrogation, no nothing. Plain and simple death.

Three of the four waited in a Ford sedan outside the apartment block. The fourth was stationed inside the building, disguised as a plumber, monitoring Akram up close. Amarjyot, in his cabin, sipped his black coffee as he got updates from the plumber, Aryaman Khanna.

Aryaman was a field officer who was cut from the same cloth as Amarjyot. A soldier with the Indian Army, Aryaman soon got recruited by the intelligence wing for his guile and grit. Truly a no-nonsense man. Unflinching when it came to taking decisions. Skilled and perceptive. Amarjyot often thought Aryaman to be a younger and certainly better version of himself.

Aryaman walked around with his plumbing toolkit past various people in the compound. He now had the necessary intelligence to move forward with the strike. He hit a button on his earpiece and spoke to Amarjyot.

'Sir, Akram is in position. We can take him out now or later when he is leaving the hotel after his night of bonking. The problem is, that might be an uncontrolled environment.'

There was a moment of silence at Amarjyot's end.

'I wouldn't want him to have any fun at all, Arya. If you take him out now, will you four be able to exit the vicinity without attracting any attention?' Amarjyot wanted to reconfirm.

'We will, sir. Jennifer is at the wheel. I can call Madhav and Randheer to take out the other boys while I deal with Akram myself.'

'Go for it,' Amarjyot said with certainty.

Inside the Ford sedan, Jennifer D'Souza smoked a cigarette nervously. Madhav Mehta, her fiancé, looked at her puffing away. He reached for the cigarette, snatched it, and dunked it into his coffee.

'You really need to stop smoking like a chimney,' Madhav said.

'It's this or a bullet.' She smiled at him. 'Or maybe once we get married, you'll want me to start again so I leave you sooner.'

'Hey lovebirds,' Randheer Bhatia said. 'Aryaman has sent his orders. We're ready to nail the bastard.'

'About time,' Jennifer murmured. 'We've been here for two weeks just watching him strut around.'

Jennifer often found surveillance the most excruciating part of espionage. Long phases of not doing anything, punctuated by a few crucial moments of actionable intelligence. Sometimes it was easy, but on a bad day it could test one's patience unbearably. Acting against the natural progression of events could blow your cover. And that, of course, could lead to the most dangerous of outcomes.

'Do we kill Akram's recruits too?' Madhav asked with a tinge of concern. 'They're kids.'

Randheer nodded as he screwed a silencer on to a pistol and handed it to Madhav.

'I don't like the idea either. But they should have known that walking down this path could get you killed any day. On their terms or ours.'

Randheer finished attaching a silencer to his own pistol just as Aryaman's voice crackled through their earpieces. Amarjyot was also on the call.

'Guys,' Aryaman said. 'This is the plan. Madhav and Randheer break in through the front door. Akram is in his room behind. His three men are outside, watching television. They are armed. So enter and finish them off immediately.'

'Copy,' Madhav and Randheer said in unison.

'On hearing the gunfire, Akram is going to escape through the window to his loo at the back, which is where I am right now, ready to take him out. Operate stealthily and we should wrap this up in three minutes flat. Jen, on my signal, bring in the car and we get the fuck out of here.'

'Sounds good, Phoenix 5,' Amarjyot concluded. 'Get to work.'

Aryaman restored the water flow in the block. It was as simple as turning a few levers to get things going.

A few hours ago, he had sneaked in through the back and turned these off. And none of the Indian residents even wanted to try to fix things themselves when they could just call a guy to do it instead.

He made his way into the three-storey building, whose ground floor Akram lived on. He walked through the dingy corridors, his silenced pistol safely tucked under his shirt and his plumbing equipment slung over his shoulder. He smiled politely at the three brown-skinned men who seemed to have stepped out of Akram's apartment itself. They eyed him suspiciously as he walked past them. Aryaman realized he hadn't seen these men before.

'Hey, you! Wait up.'

Aryaman stopped in his tracks. His earpiece was on. Jennifer, in the car, and Amarjyot, back in New Delhi, heard the unfamiliar voice. Madhav and Randheer looked at each other and knew instantly that they hadn't factored in that the building could have other sleeper agents as well.

The three men walked briskly towards Aryaman. One of them asked, 'Where do you think you're going?' Aryaman turned around to look at them, observing them for a few seconds. The one on the left was pretty scrawny, but by the way his right hand was twitching against his thigh, he looked like he was packing heat and was ready to pull out his weapon any instant. The one in the middle was a beefcake, and probably enjoyed his halal steaks and rigorous weightlifting drills at the local gym. The one on the right was tall and tough, probably the leader of the pack, since he had taken the initiative of asking Aryaman the question. Aryaman's hunch was confirmed when the tall guy took another step towards him and repeated his question: 'Where do you think you're going?'

'Sir, there seems to be some problem with the drainage in that flat.'

'Really?'

Aryaman nodded. They looked unconvinced. Then the leader turned to his two men and pointed at Aryaman's bag.

'Check his equipment,' he said softly.

Aryaman opened his bag for inspection. There was just plumbing equipment, which in Aryaman's hands was as good as a set of weapons. But he also had a gun on him. The leader told the hefty guy to frisk Aryaman. The two drew nearer to Aryaman, who had to choose between fight and flight now. As the big guy inched closer, Aryaman made up his mind. He was going to make the first move and be on top of things.

He stepped back, crouched swiftly, pulled his gun out and shot the big guy square in the head. The scrawny man pulled out his weapon and took aim, but Aryaman dropped flat to the ground and fired at his kneecap. The man let out a yelp, and the next bullet went into his skull. The leader was swift to react. He picked up the gun from the floor and fired three quick rounds at Aryaman, who rolled to his left. One bullet scraped his shoulder, causing him to drop his weapon.

Now that he had no chance of getting to his gun, he ran head first at the guy and rammed him into the wall. The man threw punches at Aryaman so he could push him back and take a shot at him, but Aryaman blocked the punches with his forearms. Before the man could try to fire at him, Aryaman twisted his arm, seized the gun out of his hand, and shot him in the head, sending blood splattering all over the wall.

Realizing that the gunshots may have led Akram to flee, Aryaman ran towards the door, talking into his earpiece. 'Randheer! Madhav! Get to the back! Akram will try to escape!'

Amarjyot listened in with bated breath. He had not expected such a solid counterattack. 'Randheer, I suggest you stay back in the building and help Aryaman. There could be reinforcements coming in from the floors above. Madhav and Jennifer, if you see Akram outside, shoot to kill! Don't worry about witnesses!'

'Copy sir,' Jennifer said, driving the car into the compound and abandoning all attempts at subtlety now. The rain began to beat down harder on the ground and people had moved indoors, so there weren't too many witnesses around anyway.

Aryaman fired at the lock and kicked the door down. Randheer entered the corridor, catching up with him. The three recruits were waiting with their guns at the ready. They opened fire at Aryaman, who ran back into the corridor to take cover and saw the recruits charging forward. Randheer fired from behind the recruits, sending a bullet through one recruit's breastbone.

The other two hesitated at the sight of their dead friend. Aryaman saw the opportunity and exposed himself for a split second. One recruit lifted his gun to fire at him, but Aryaman dropped to his knees and took his shot. The bullet pierced the man's neck through and through, jerking his head back. His injured friend decided to make a run for it; like his boss, he wasn't ready for heaven just yet.

The recruit entered the bathroom and saw the open skylight window through which Akram had hastily escaped. He stepped on to the washbasin, propping himself up, so he could jump out. He attempted to launch himself out, but Aryaman grabbed his leg and dragged him back inside, making him fall face first. The man was badly injured, but there was still some life left in him. Aryaman lifted him up, smashed his head into the mirror and then on the washbasin. With a thick piece of ceramic tile, Aryaman stabbed the man in the hollow below his Adam's apple and wrenched it hard. He watched the horror in the recruit's eyes as life slipped out of him.

Moments later, Aryaman and Randheer heard footsteps hurrying towards them.

'They've got backup,' Aryaman said. 'Come on, Randheer, climb on my back and get out of here.'

'Aren't you coming?'

'After you,' Aryaman replied as he helped Randheer out of the bathroom. Randheer dropped a few feet to the ground outside and helped Aryaman climb out next. The bullet wound in Aryaman's shoulder shot an electric pain through his body, but he managed anyway, lacking his usual grace though still as effective.

Outside, Akram was adjusting his jacket, holding his gun at the ready. He saw Madhav approaching him. In the car, Jennifer sped towards Akram to run him over, but his reflexes were surprisingly good. He threw himself to the side and began firing at her. A bullet hit the windscreen, missing her by a few inches. Her vehicle swerved and hit a wall. The airbags burst open, and she was disoriented.

Akram ran towards her car, aiming his gun at Jennifer's head. From a distance, Madhav raised his gun to fire at Akram.

'Stop or I shoot!' Madhav said.

Akram froze as Madhav began to approach him. The residents of the neighbourhood watched everything from behind closed windows, panic and fear writ large on their faces. They had already called the cops.

Madhav moved cautiously towards Akram, who took a step towards Jennifer. She was still dizzy from the impact of the car crash. Randheer and Aryaman rushed to the spot.

'Shoot her and you're dead, Akram!' Madhav growled. 'Walk away. This is your chance.'

'You Indians don't learn, do you?' Akram grinned, his finger firmly placed on the trigger of the gun aimed at Jennifer. 'Death doesn't inspire fear in our hearts the way it does in yours.'

Aryaman assessed the situation as an agitated Amarjyot asked him for an update.

'For God's sake, sir. Hold on,' he muttered into the earpiece.

Randheer's hands were shaking in agitation. He spotted two more of what he rightly presumed to be Akram's men running towards them. Swiftly taking aim, he shot them both dead before they could react.

Akram had heard the gunshots. He looked at Madhav and then at Jennifer, who had come to her senses and was reaching for her gun. On impulse, Akram pulled the trigger.

Things slowed before Madhav's eyes as he saw Jennifer's brains blown to bits, staining the interior of the car. He yelled out in pain as he watched the love of his life die. He pointed his gun and fired at Akram, who had run for cover behind the car. Madhav followed him furiously.

Aryaman and Randheer ran after him. And then Aryaman saw it: the jacket. Akram didn't have it on earlier, when they were tracking him. The jacket was wired to explosives. Aryaman took Randheer by the arm and pulled him back towards him.

'Madhav, stay back!'

But it was too late. Aryaman saw Akram press the button of the detonator that he'd pulled out of his jacket's front pocket.

'Allahu Akbar!' Akram yelled one final time.

A deafening explosion rocked the neighbourhood. Fire engulfed Madhav. Aryaman and Randheer were flung backwards. After a short while, Aryaman tried to get to his feet but struggled to do so. He saw Madhav's charred body, still ablaze. Where Akram was supposed to be standing there were bits of flesh mangled with metal from the destroyed car. Aryaman's vision began to fade as he inhaled the toxic black smoke.

'Sir, they are gone. Jen. Madhav. Gone . . .' Aryaman lost consciousness.

Amarjyot buried his head in his hands. Failure had met them when they least expected it. Akram was gone. But was this a victory when two of his best agents were dead? He sank back in his chair, feeling nauseated. He couldn't even share his burden. There'd be a price to pay if he were to walk into his boss's cabin and tell him about the unsanctioned operation going south.

Two Days Later: New Delhi, IRW HQ

Amarjyot's boss Ashish Singh was furious upon learning what had transpired. He looked distraught, scratching his bald head. There was just Amarjyot with him in his cabin, which housed various medals and certificates he had received in his career. He looked up at the screen that displayed a paused smartphone video of the Southall incident, shot by an onlooker. The grainy footage had found its way to mainstream media and was being broadcast all over the world. Amarjyot had a blank expression on his hardened, aged face.

'Two of our agents, dead in public view.'

'Maqsood Akram dead too. Don't forget that, sir.'

Singh played the video again. They saw Akram pressing the detonator.

'He killed himself,' Singh said. 'Your men didn't do it. He will go down as a hero for the jihadis waiting to join the fight.'

'Sir? With all due respect, can you hear how ridiculous you sound?'

Singh did not take this well. He leaned forward. And Amarjyot, not one to back down easily, mirrored his boss's body language.

'Bipin has briefed me about this Phoenix 5 business, Amarjyot. This is what happens when you start thinking you are above the law.'

'Bipin wants my job, sir. So he could bring his spinelessness to bear on the important decisions that we have to make as guardians of the country.'

Amarjyot's sarcasm wasn't lost on Singh.

'Nevertheless,' Singh said. 'You have acted of your own volition. Your two boys, Aryaman and Randheer, will get the punishment that is due to them as well. There will be a formal inquiry.'

Amarjyot slammed the table and stood up.

'The Phoenix 5 has been active for only a short span of time and has been successful on numerous occasions, sir. What about those? The one time we "fail"—which is how you insist on looking at it—you want to crucify us? We took out a major enemy of the country. So what if there's a damn clip circulating on social media?'

'And Madhav and Jennifer?'

'I hate the fact that we lost them,' Amarjyot said gravely. 'But they were soldiers. They knew what they were signing up for. If they wanted to play it safe, they would have opted to become bureaucrats like you and that fucking Bipin Sharma.'

Amarjyot stormed out of the room, banging the door shut behind him. Singh knew that Amarjyot wasn't one for theatrics and that this operation had really affected him. But this was impertinence of the highest kind. He wouldn't react to it now. There would be an inquiry in a couple of days, he thought. Amarjyot would be history after that.

On the morning of the inquiry, Amarjyot woke up with a terrible headache. The last two days had been a nightmare for him, and he had relied on large volumes of alcohol to divert his mind and to put himself to sleep. He knew what was coming his way. He was going to be discharged and stripped of his rank. A lifetime of dedication towards his country had trickled down to this. A ceremony of humiliation.

He struggled to get out of bed. His wife, Savita, walked in with a cup of tea. She had tears in her eyes when she saw her husband distraught. He looked at the cup of tea and shook his head. She sat beside him. Their son, Abhay, watched this for a few moments before stepping into the room.

'It's over, Savita.'

'Don't say that. You did all you could and more. The country doesn't deserve you.'

'The country deserves more. I just tried to push myself to that limit. All five of us believed we could make a change. Such fucking fools. And now some stupid bastard is going to pass judgement on my contributions. And some other fool is going to replace me. All that I did, I did honourably. But they won't see it that way.'

His voice trailed away as he burst into tears. The seventeen-year-old Abhay, too young to know how to react, sat by his father's shivering feet.

'I can't take this humiliation,' Amarjyot cried. 'I won't allow it.'

Savita hugged him, letting him sob. Abhay pressed his father's legs softly, wondering how a war hero could be reduced to this.

Amarjyot sat up straight, wiping his tears.

'I need some paracetamol,' he said. 'I feel a fever coming on. I looked for some last night, but we are out of the tablets. Can you go and buy some?' At this, Abhay obediently walked out of the room.

'Savita, I'll be fine,' Amarjyot stood up, taking a sip of tea. 'Go with Abhay. Speak to him. Get some fresh air. This shouldn't affect him. He's too young.'

Savita looked at him, tears in her eyes. She stood up to walk away, trying hard to put on a smile.

'We'll be back in ten minutes,' she said. 'Freshen up, and then we'll eat breakfast together.'

Amarjyot nodded. She walked up to him and, bending a little, pecked him tenderly on the forehead. He smiled as he watched her leave.

He stood by the window, watching his wife and son speak animatedly as they walked to the chemist's at the end of the lane. He turned around and walked to his closet with great resolve. He opened it and unlocked his safe with the passcode that only he knew. The safe carried a few important documents, a few gadgets and a gun.

He didn't wait another moment. He already knew what people were going to say. Some would call him a coward; others would take his name with great respect for his contribution to the realm of Indian intelligence. He did not want to be at the receiving end of an inquiry where all his detractors scavenged off his remains. For him, this was the only way to save face.

He raised the gun to his temple and looked, one last time, at the family photo propped up on his desk. He would be a burden to his wife if he was chucked out of the agency. Even she knew she came a close second to his job. A close second but still second. Hopefully, his son would be dissuaded from following in his father's footsteps, dissuaded from joining the military or espionage agencies. And that would be a great thing for him. Amarjyot Bhushan closed his eyes and took in a deep breath. His last.

Then he pulled the trigger.

At the inquiry later that day, the third chair that was meant for Amarjyot Bhushan remained empty. Bipin Sharma had walked in early, his mousy features not contorting even to feign remorse for Amarjyot's death. Chief Ashish Singh looked adequately affected when he took his seat. He had never expected this of Amarjyot. He learnt the news about an hour after the body was discovered by Amarjyot's wife and son. It jolted him in a way he never thought anything could.

Aryaman's straight, black hair was tousled, and his eyes were bloodshot when he was brought in to sit before Singh and Sharma. His shirt was buttoned up all wrong, and he reeked of cigarettes. He stared at the ground.

Randheer, his head hanging in shame, was brought into the stuffy room by a young guard.

'Okay,' Sharma said. 'Aryaman, we want to hear your version of the story first. Go on.'

Aryaman cast a sideways glance at Amarjyot's chair and then at a crestfallen Randheer. He turned to Sharma defiantly.

'Bipin Sir, I know you are itching to get into Amarjyot's shoes. But maybe we can hold on for a few minutes and wait for him to join us before we start the grilling?'

There was silence. Ashish Singh looked at Bipin Sharma and then nodded curtly, as if to say, 'Let me handle this.' He then turned his gaze to a confused Randheer and an adamant-looking Aryaman.

'Amarjyot Bhushan was found dead at his residence earlier this morning,' he said flatly. 'Suicide. No signs of foul play. Shot himself.'

The words lingered in the air. Randheer broke down instantly, tears streaming out, his body shaking with soft sobs. Aryaman let the fact sink in. He could feel his heart pounding against his ribcage, his teeth grinding, his jaw hardening. Fighting back the urge to yell out angrily or burst into tears, all he could feebly manage were two words.

'Well, then,' he said, softly.

'Shall we proceed?' Sharma asked.

Aryaman looked at Randheer and nodded.

'Randheer had nothing to do with this,' Aryaman said. 'As far as Randheer, Madhav and Jennifer were concerned, they didn't know the mission was unsanctioned.'

'You liar!' Sharma raised his voice.

Singh appealed for calm with a gesture towards Sharma. Randheer looked taken aback at what Aryaman had just said. He was about to speak when Aryaman shot him one stern glance that implied, 'Don't even think about it.'

'If we are getting into name-calling, maybe I should call you an opportunist too, Bipin Sir.'

'Aryaman,' Singh said to defuse the situation. 'Carry on with your deposition. If what you are saying is indeed true, the blame falls squarely on you and Amarjyot.'

'The other three were young and impressionable,' Aryaman continued. 'Amarjyot Sir was in his early sixties. I am in my mid-forties. We were their seniors. Age- and rank-wise. They believed what we said blindly.'

'And the Phoenix 5?' Sharma spluttered.

'A fancy name Amarjyot Sir and I made up just to make it seem like this whole thing was official. Again, I state that the other three had nothing to do with it. They were misled by Amarjyot Bhushan and me into becoming a part of these unsanctioned operations.'

Both Singh and Sharma looked helpless. Aryaman seemed determined to sell them this story. They looked at Randheer.

Sharma addressed him. 'Is this true? You had no knowledge that these operations were unsanctioned?'

Randheer felt his face going numb. Aryaman turned towards him, expecting him to back the lie. Randheer heard the question being repeated.

'Yes,' he said, after what seemed like an eternity. 'I had no knowledge about these operations being unsanctioned.'

He turned to look at Aryaman, who had slumped back into his chair. Expressionless.

'Then in that case,' Singh said with an air of finality, 'Randheer, you will be limited to being a desk agent after six months of suspension.'

Randheer was being let off easily and even he knew it. The attention shifted to Aryaman.

'As for you,' Singh continued. 'Seven years of rigorous imprisonment at the Quarry in Lakshadweep.'

Aryaman nodded and said, 'May Amarjyot Bhushan's soul rest in peace.' He then stood up to be led away.

2

Her eyes had a lot to say. They let on more than she ever did with her words. He was her husband. He was the father of their child. But even then, there were things about her he did not know. She had opened up as much as she could have, but some things had never been expressed in words. He would often think of those things. And he had a strong hunch what they could have been. He was a spy after all.

She was protective of their son to the point of obsession. Things that she would say to him would surprise him sometimes. He would always reassure her that the environment their son was growing up in was secure.

'That's where you're wrong,' she would say with an air of finality.

He knew his wife had been abused as a child. And he knew it was her father. For a person brimming with love, his wife despised the man responsible for her existence with a caustic hatred. Her father pretended never to know why, but he did, although he never spoke to her about it. She did not want to attend his last rites when he passed away. She never said why.

Aryaman remembered the first time they made love. The scent in her wild hair. Her full lips against his. It was on their third date. She didn't know about his actual work until they were married. She wasn't completely surprised, though. Her line of work involved fraternizing with men like him. And she had always suspected he belonged to the shadowy world of espionage. But there was an honesty about him that made her fall for him. Honesty and resolve that saw them through some difficult times. Their first child was stillborn. The news had shattered them. They were luckier the next time, a couple of years later. Blessed with a baby boy, they finally got to know real happiness. He made her feel safe. And she made him feel safe too. This was how it was meant to be. But not for long . . .

His son must have turned fifteen now. The last time he had seen him, he was just seven. He knew, too, that his wife must have changed. But he hoped and prayed that her compassion for him had remained. He had spent years trying to imagine what she must have gone through. If she were to tell him she loathes him, he'd understand. It would have been tough to raise a child without being able to justify the father's disappearance. She had been through a lot. He was supposed to step in and make things right. Instead, he had made them worse.

He had had no contact with the external world. No man was tough enough to go through this. He longed for her more than for anything else. And in ways that transcended physical intimacy. She was his support system, even if he hadn't seen her all this while.

There were butterflies in his stomach. He was about to go back to his family—his wife and son—soon. And his mother? He didn't know if she was still alive. The prisoners were usually intimated about the death of a family member, but sometimes the messages didn't get through in time. Bureaucracy everywhere. It scared him each time he thought about getting out. He felt as though a hand had grabbed him by the throat and was choking him. Maybe he was better off in this shithole, not seeing his family, not knowing what was happening to them; this was better than realizing his worst fears had been confirmed. By now, they had probably got used to living without him. Why shake things up now . . .

Clang!

The noise broke his chain of thoughts. It was time.

A plate came sliding against the ground and hit his head. He sat up, squinting at the little opening through which a man stared at him.

'Last day today?'

A bare-bodied Aryaman, wearing nothing save for a pair of boxers, sat up on his haunches. He noticed the man's clean-shaven face and neat haircut.

'Is it your first?' he asked in his gravelly voice.

The man nodded.

'I've heard stories about you,' the guard said. 'If left to me, I wouldn't have had you imprisoned. And definitely not here.'

Aryaman smiled as he picked up the sticky rice from the plate and swallowed it without chewing. Some of it got stuck in his grimy, long beard.

'Well, if things were left up to you or me, the world would have been a different place.'

The guard's face softened. 'Well, have your meal. And then shower and get ready to leave. You have an hour.'

'Thanks, kid.'

The opening in the door clamped up, rendering the room dark again except for a few rays of sunlight. Aryaman polished the food off his plate as he watched the dancing specks of dust in the light. He looked at the drab walls with the paint peeling off; the single mattress that he would roll up and use as a punching bag during the day; the unsteady commode that barely functioned. All witnesses to his last seven years of existence.

The door slid open again. The guard picked up the plate and then scrutinized Aryaman's chiselled body, aged and scarred, though solid. The cell door was opened all the way and Aryaman stepped out.

He was led to the common shower area. Aryaman stepped in while the guard stayed back at the door.

There was a group of inmates already here. Most of them were stark naked, singing and cracking crude jokes at the top of their voices. He stood under a shower and disrobed.

In prison, he had rubbed shoulders, sometimes literally, with the scum of the earth. International terrorists, gun runners, drug dealers, murderers, all of whom the Indian authorities had captured in covert missions and imprisoned. Aryaman had never imagined breaking bread with the very men he was trained to bring to book. But this was where circumstances had led him.

On his first day in prison, he caught the attention of one Afghani warlord, who had been captured in Kandahar. The warlord, a bit of a bully, commanded the respect of many of the Muslim inmates. A few days into his jail sentence, Aryaman was ambushed at the dinner table. Caught unawares, he was thrashed severely with metal plates and cutlery, and was dragged to the warlord, who had begun to take his pants off so he could sodomize Aryaman.

But little did the bully know that he would have to pay dearly for this.

Aryaman, having recovered from the thrashing somewhat, got to his feet. Before the warlord could bat an eyelid, his two lackeys were flat on the ground, knocked out. One of them had made the mistake of carrying the fork which was used to scar Aryaman's back earlier. Aryaman grabbed this fork and stabbed the warlord in his eye and kicked him in the groin. The warlord slumped to the ground, blacking out instantly.

That was that. Nobody ever messed with Aryaman in the jail again.

Now here he was, having his last shower at the prison. The hot water dripped down his largely grey, tangled hair and ran down his chest. He rinsed himself thoroughly, thinking of starting life afresh. As if it were that simple!

He was trying to ignore the crude conversations of his fellow inmates but something caught his ear.

'The new kid,' one tattooed bully scoffed. 'Time to initiate him into our world.'

'A fine piece of ass,' said his friend, a bearded hulk of a man. 'Waiting for us.'

Aryaman finished his shower and towelled himself dry. They would overpower him in no time, he thought. The guard was patiently standing at the door, waiting for him to finish.

'Leave the kid alone,' Aryaman said, wrapping the towel around his waist. 'Why don't you two just fuck each other instead, until your assholes bleed?'

The two men looked at him, taken aback. They were going to have none of it.

'What do you care?' one of them growled.

'Isn't it your last day?' the other one chimed in. 'Do you want to go out on a wheelchair? Or even worse, a stretcher?'

Aryaman shrugged as he walked towards the exit.

'Just a friendly warning,' he said softly. 'Leave the kid alone.'

The bearded man towered over him, blocking his way.

'You know, I often wonder if any of those stories about you are true. Are you that tough? Or is it a myth spread by your people, so that nobody touches you? Because you're still a government employee after all.'

Aryaman met him with a piercing glare, but addressed the other guy.

'Why don't you come and take your friend away before you both find out whether what they say about me is a myth?'

The other man walked towards Aryaman, but not to take his friend away. It was now two against one.

'Guess you're going to find out then,' Aryaman said, icily.

Aryaman had spent enough time in the prison's shower area to know about the seemingly innocuous things that could be used as weapons. He was always ready. For someone built like Aryaman, muscle-flexing was not much of an option. He would have to let his agility and swiftness take charge. He would wait for them to make their first move, after which he would slide on the slippery floor towards the washbasin and mirror. That would be an advantageous spot to station himself, in order to limit a frontal assault and take his assailants by surprise.

It usually takes five seconds to understand an opponent. But Aryaman didn't even need that. He instantly knew the big guy was going to take the first shot at him. And so it was. Just as the big guy threw a punch with his right arm, Aryaman dropped to his knees and propelled himself forward on the slippery floor through the gap between the two men. Both of them took a second to turn around. Enraged, they let out a yell and charged at him. Aryaman ripped the mirror panel off the wall and sent it crashing into the big guy's skull. With the remaining shards of glass in his hand, he slashed hard at the other man's bare chest.

A few sharp pieces of glass were lodged in his arm, but he ignored the pain. He bent over and punched one of them repeatedly on the face, reducing his nose to a bloody pulp. The other guy was still reeling from the attack with the mirror.

Blood, mixed with water, streamed towards the drain. Aryaman stood up, looking at the two men he had floored. He was panting, which surprised him. The years had taken their toll. When he was younger, this was barely enough combat to get him warmed up, much less tired. He caught his breath and walked to the door, which he knocked sharply. The guard turned his gaze towards him, nodded once and opened the door. He looked at the mess behind Aryaman, appalled.

'Saved your ass,' Aryaman said. 'Quite literally.'

Aryaman walked past him nonchalantly. The guard looked at the two men still writhing in pain. He then turned to Aryaman and asked, 'What did they do?'

'Wanted to "initiate" you,' Aryaman said, sounding tired. 'Their words, not mine.'

He walked to a mirror and began combing his beard with his fingers. The guard still seemed frozen in his place.

'They're not dead,' Aryaman continued. 'Don't worry.'

The guard nodded nervously. His eyes followed Aryaman.

'I wouldn't mind a thank you,' Aryaman said. 'But who's complaining.'

The guard didn't respond. And after a brief pause, he said, 'You can change into your civilian clothes. You will leave in an hour, after the paperwork is taken care of. I believe your mother is outside, waiting for you.' He then left, to clean up the mess in the shower area.

Aryaman looked at his cragged, lined face in the mirror. His mother was alive after all. But was any part of his old self still there for her to recognize?

3

Few islands in Lakshadweep have human habitations. Fewer still are open to visitors and tourists. The island that housed the maximum security prison, the Quarry, was certainly off limits to one and all.

Aryaman put on the simple white shirt and starched trousers that the jail authorities had provided him with. Accompanied by the young guard and two other officials, he stepped out of the prison gates. He squinted at his surroundings, the sun hitting him hard in the face. He hadn't been in an area this open for quite a while.

'Got a smoke?'

The young guy nodded.

'Care to give me one?'

The other two officials were eying the guard accusingly.

'I'm sorry, I can't . . .'

Aryaman sighed and started walking down the path that led to a small motorboat, which would transfer him to the island where his mother was waiting. The two officials got on the boat first. They stood straight, at attention. From the cold expression on their faces, they seemed ready to use their guns in case he did anything untoward. Why they thought he would do so was beyond him.

As Aryaman got on board, the young guard extended his arm for a valedictory handshake. Aryaman was slow to respond, but he felt a cigarette and matchbox being pressed into his palm. He concealed them in his pocket and, smiling to himself, took his seat.

The boat began to speed towards the other island, which didn't seem very far. The blue water, the strong gusts of wind, and the greenness at the shore—all felt so unreal, worlds away from what Aryaman had got used to. So alien. He took in a lungful of air and closed his eyes. The two officials were observing him closely.

'Just out of curiosity,' Aryaman addressed them. 'Had that kid passed me a cigarette, would he have lost his job?'

The officials shrugged as though in unison.

'Not really,' one of them said curtly. 'But isn't it highly unprofessional? I mean, I wouldn't go handing over cigarettes to criminals who want to bum smokes off me.'

The word 'criminal' seemed to linger in the air. Aryaman struck a matchstick against the box and lit his cigarette.

'Criminality comes in all shapes and sizes,' he said. 'The guys you work for are bigger criminals than I am. Go shoot your mouths off there.'

The rest of the trip passed in silence. The man in charge of navigation pulled up at the island and anchored the boat. Aryaman stepped out and walked with short but assertive strides on the sand. He took in one last drag and dropped the cigarette on the beach.

The two officials led him through a pathway flanked by trees. He walked behind them, trying to take in the beauty of the land where he had been imprisoned. But strangely, he felt nothing. He was a free man now. He wanted to feel something. Anything. His mind soon complied, but he wasn't thinking about himself. Rather, he thought of Amarjyot Bhushan; of Amarjyot's son and wife, not of his own son and wife. He thought of the other deceased members of the Phoenix 5, Madhav and Jennifer; not of his own deceased father. He thought of Randheer; not of his friends.

They entered a little shed. There were a few chairs and a large table with documents laid out on it.

One of the officials pointed at a chair. 'Take a seat, Mr Khanna.'

Aryaman sat down, but not on the chair the official had pointed at.

'We are going to bring in an analyst to evaluate your physiological and psychological condition before we transfer you to Delhi.'

'What's the point?' Aryaman snapped. 'I am not joining the agency again. What do you guys care about my mental or physical state?'

'It's a formality unless you show signs of extremely disturbing behaviour,' the official said. 'Besides, we don't particularly care. The system does.'

'Pretends to care,' Aryaman resumed. 'Get this damn formality done with. I want to see my mother. Send her in.'

'After the psychiatrist evaluates you, I'm afraid.'

The officials stepped out of the shed. Moments later, a distinguished-looking elderly man walked in. He took his seat across the table from Aryaman, who lay slumped defiantly on his chair and did not make eye contact with the psychiatrist.

'I understand why you are not keen to go through this.'

'Do you?' Aryaman stared at the ceiling. 'Is anybody ever keen to go through this?'

There was a cold silence. Aryaman shifted his gaze to the psychiatrist.

'Let's go through this, sir.'

The psychiatrist switched on a tape recorder. Aryaman was eyeing it with contempt.

'For the record, I am Dr Bhupendra Varma, the in-house psychiatrist with the IRW,' the psychiatrist said.

'My subject today is Mr Aryaman Khanna, just released from the Quarry. To be determined whether he's fit to resume life as a civilian or requires special rehabilitation.'

Aryaman let out a derisive laugh.

'Tell us about your stay at the Quarry, Mr Khanna.'

Aryaman knew the drill. They would ask him standard questions. Seemingly innocuous. Borderline funny, even. If he lost his mind at any point . . . But he would have to be in control. He shouldn't let this get to him. He shouldn't snap. Because that would mean months at a rehab centre. And honestly, he would prefer returning to the Quarry instead.

'I have stayed in better conditions,' Aryaman said, straight-faced.

'Did you make friends there?'

'I don't make friends easily.'

'And why is that?'

'Trust is a currency we don't part with too generously in the world of intelligence.'

Varma nodded and pursed his lips.

'Have you ever had suicidal thoughts?'

'No.' Aryaman once again avoided eye contact.

'None at all?' the psychiatrist asked, writing something down in his notebook.

'Well,' Aryaman said softly, 'I did think of violence a lot. But not of inflicting it upon myself.'

'And who was the recipient of your violence?'

Aryaman grinned. 'Your bosses wouldn't like to hear their names spoken in this regard. So I would not like to cross that line. Honestly, I don't think I need rehab.'

'That's for us to decide.'

There was an element of certainty in Varma's voice. He offered a glass of water to Aryaman—probably an olive branch—but Aryaman refused it.

'So what did you spend most of your time thinking about in the Quarry?'

'The usual.'

'Your wife? Your kid? Your mother?'

Aryaman nodded. But that wasn't the whole truth. He had spent most of his time thinking about the incident in London; about where it all went wrong.

'I think about my country.' Aryaman's hands began to tremble, partly in fear, partly in rage. 'I think about everything we did for it. Amarjyot Sir. Jennifer and Madhav. Randheer. Myself. We put everything on the line to take decisions that the men in charge didn't have the spine to take.'

'Isn't that unfair? Isn't that a myopic way of looking at justice?'

'Then tell me a good way of meting out justice to a bastard like Maqsood Akram. Is there one?'

There was no response.

'I thought as much,' Aryaman said, now red with rage. 'I spent years in that damn shithole for an act that your superiors may have very well gloated over after doling out their warped version of justice. The world would have celebrated the death of that scumbag Akram. Your bosses must have clinked flutes of champagne to a victory that was actually the Phoenix 5's. That was actually the victory of Amarjyot Singh.'

Varma prodded him further. 'Do you want to say more?'

'To what effect?' Aryaman stood up. 'To be called clinically insane? To be tossed into another unhealthy environment where people who have no clue about my life will tell me how to rebuild it? Fuck that. I am sane enough not to snap your neck and leave right now. That should help you make your decision.'

Aryaman walked out of the shed, knowing full well that this could work against him. But he was in no mood for nonsense. He glared at the two officials, who seemed intimidated by his body language.

He walked past them back towards the beach, but they followed closely behind.

'Stay the fuck away,' he growled.

He was heading out for the sea when he lost his balance and fell, not far from the shoreline. His eyes welled up as he stared at the water. Eventually, the sound of waves breaking against the shore soothed him.

Back in the tent, Bhupendra Varma made a call to Bipin Sharma.

'It went as expected, sir. He's bitter for sure. But not incoherent or insane.'

Varma interrupted himself to down a glass of water.

'Yes,' he continued. 'You could probably keep him under surveillance for a month to determine his behaviour. But I think that would a waste of time. He'll work his way into normality once he meets his mother. His wife. His kid. He seems like a guy who can bounce back.'

Aarti Singh was often told that she was a brave woman. Some even said that she had the strength and endurance of a man. And she hated that. It irked her that her qualities were defined in relation to those of the opposite sex. In fact, she would argue, women were stronger than men. Most men she said this to would snigger and not pursue the argument any further. Such was the nature of the world she had chosen to work in.

Aarti was with the Indian Army Medical Corps, the unit that primarily provided medical services to soldiers—both serving and veteran—and to their families. For a large part of her career, she had been posted in Kashmir. She was made to work in tandem with active IRW agents, providing them with healthcare aid when required. In those days, she had met an agent, Suryaveer Khanna, who had been severely injured in combat. Suryaveer was on the verge of death when she first saw him. He was rescued in time, but his injuries were severe. It was Aarti who cared for him in those days and nursed him back to health. Neither of them could help falling in love with each other.

Soon after, their stint in Kashmir over, they returned to Delhi and got married. Aarti was pregnant a year later, but fate played its cards. Suryaveer was called back on an urgent mission in Kashmir. He thought of opting out of it, but Aarti pushed him into going.

'By the time you're done,' she said with a gentle smile, 'our baby will be born.'

So Suryaveer went to war, and he never came back. He died in a bomb blast. His body, Aarti was told, was never recovered from the site of the blast; there was probably nothing left of him. She remembered hearing the news from Suryaveer's colleagues, their faces grave. Her response had been to gently close the door on them, having acknowledged them with a nod and thanked them for bearing the news with such dignity. She walked towards the cradle that held her newborn son and watched him as he joyously flailed his arms. Then, she allowed herself to break down. Maybe this was her fault. She had sent her husband, the man she loved more than anyone else, to his death. Her unnamed son had been left without a father. She wanted them to name the child together. But that wasn't to be. In a moment of weakness, she cursed herself and smashed an ashtray against the wall. The baby remained unfazed. She sat at the edge of the bed and calmed herself down. If she could, she thought, she would do it again. She would sacrifice love for the nation. Her father had served the nation. She had served the nation. Her husband had served the nation. Soon, her son would follow in their footsteps.

She lifted the baby in her arms and looked at his smiling face with great resolve. That moment she decided to name him Aryaman—a Sanskrit word that loosely translates to 'companion'—since he was all she had.

Aarti Khanna was waiting patiently for her son. She had been given the option of meeting him in Delhi, but she insisted on flying down to Lakshadweep. Ashish Singh, who knew of the sacrifices she had made for the nation, did not want to deny her this small request.

Aarti wore a salwar kameez and had cut her grey hair short. She walked with a slight limp. Despite what she had gone through in life, she came across as an optimistic person, always meeting people with her courteous, disarming smile.

Awaiting the return of her brave son, Aarti felt a sense of pride. Aryaman was a man of great integrity. His colleague Randheer had met her after the sentencing and had told her everything. Reporting the facts, Randheer had broken down, and she had consoled him like a mother. She had explained that Aryaman's resolve came from his father. 'It is hereditary,' she joked. But Randheer could see that Aryaman was just like his mother.

Aryaman entered the makeshift shed and walked up to his mother. She examined him. He was the spitting image of his dad. She held him tight, locking him in an embrace that moved him to tears.

'I'm sorry, Ma. I didn't mean to make you wait this long.'

She cut short the hug and slapped him lightly on the cheek.

'Arya, don't say that. I would have been disappointed if you had taken the easy route out of this one.'

Aryaman kissed her on the forehead. Time had done her no favours and the marks were visible on her aged face. He noticed her eyes behind her spectacles. They were beginning to grow milky. Probably a cataract on its way. It broke Aryaman's heart. She wiped his tears, and he embraced her again.

As Aryaman signed the papers and completed the formalities, she watched him with great fondness. This was just the reunion she'd imagined. Unlike the one she had hoped for years ago with her husband.

They were led to another boat. This time, they were going to the airport situated on Agatti Island.

'So,' she continued as the boat began to move. 'Jyoti's been waiting for you. Reach Delhi and call her up. And then take the flight to Mumbai tomorrow. Your son needs to be with his father. Family is all you have, Aryaman. It took me years to understand that.'

'And they are all I need, Ma. The rest of my life will only be devoted to them,' Aryaman said with a lump in his throat.

4

The *Indian Daily Report* newsroom was buzzing with chatter and frenetic activity. Several junior journalists lined up outside senior editor Jyoti Khanna's cabin, their stories printed out and ready to be submitted for her approval. Jyoti, however, was busy on a phone call. She had gestured fifteen minutes ago for them to hang on until she was done. And they had been waiting patiently since.

They chatted about her while she seemed deep in conversation. Everyone discussed how she hadn't left her cabin all day, wondering what secret story she was working on. None of them had a clue. Except for the prematurely grey-haired thirty-two-year-old Ehsaan Qureshi, a senior journalist and her closest friend. He ignored everyone, his lanky frame bent over the papers on his desk. She had been working with him all day.

Everyone admired Jyoti's integrity. People looked up to her for her unrelenting commitment to, and passion for, her work. She could be hard-nosed about certain things, but only at work. When she met someone in her off-hours—when, say, she was grabbing a drink post-work—she was a delight.

With Jyoti still on the call, some of them looked expectantly at Ehsaan. He was not his usual jovial self today. He came to the door, shrugged and said in a flat tone, 'She'll get done and call you guys inside. Get back to your desks.' They slowly dispersed.

Inside her cabin, Jyoti was fighting a battle of her own. Two battles actually. One was work-related. An explosive story had landed in her lap. She had spent the past week researching it with Ehsaan. Only he knew about it, and it would have major implications once she filed it later that night. She had kept the presses waiting.

Her second battle was personal: speaking to the man she had once known as her husband. On paper, he still was. But the time they had spent apart had damaged their relationship beyond repair. Or so she thought. There were moments she had almost strayed. She had almost succumbed to her desire—the desire to be with another man. It was part of being human, she told herself. This need for someone to fill the void that her husband had left behind. But she couldn't get herself to do it. She loved her husband too much to let another relationship get in the way of the bond she shared with him. Instead, she devoted herself wholeheartedly to her work, and to her son.

Hearing his gravelly voice on the phone almost made her forget the anger and irritation she felt towards him. She knew she was still his. These were feelings that would never go away.

His voice sounded like it had changed a bit, so she could only imagine what he looked like. Probably haggard and forlorn. His cheeks must have sunk. His hair must have greyed. His eyes must have lost the spark they once carried. And now he was on the phone telling her that he would see her the next morning. That he would come back and make it right.

'I could keep apologizing,' Aryaman said. 'But that's not going to change a thing. I will come back and set things right. I'll be the husband you missed. And I'll be the father Aditya needs.'

'When can I expect you?' she asked, almost choking up.

'Tomorrow,' he said. 'There are some formalities that I have to take care of in Delhi before I fly into Mumbai. I'll take the first flight tomorrow. Mother will come with me.'

'I know,' Jyoti said. 'She'd been following up with Delhi every day for the last month. She insisted on flying out to see you. They didn't allow me to come. So she flew from Dehradun to Delhi herself, and then they took her to Lakshadweep.'

She could hear Aryaman sighing.

'Arya?' she asked.

'Your love and hers kept me going, Jyoti. I will see you tomorrow.'

He hung up. To Jyoti, his voice sounded like he was crying. She had seen him cry a few times. He was extremely vulnerable despite the tough exterior. Besides, his job wasn't easy. The stakes were always high. It was like walking a tightrope every waking moment. A slight misstep could plunge you into hell. And that's exactly what had happened to him. She was glad he was going to get another stab at life. And she had to be there for him, to help him resurrect himself.

She got up from her desk and walked out of the newsroom. Glancing at her watch, she realized why her team appeared worried. They were past the deadline. She looked at Ehsaan and motioned for him to enter the cabin. In the direction of the other journalists, who were gazing at her expectantly, she merely held up the palm of her hand as a signal to wait.

Ehsaan stepped in, closing the door behind him.

'Ehsaan,' Jyoti said, crashing into her chair. 'Arya is back. He is meeting us tomorrow.'

There were beads of sweat on her forehead despite the air-conditioning.

'Well,' Ehsaan said softly. 'It's overwhelming, certainly. You need a break, Jyoti. Fuck this case. It's taking a toll on you. Get back to your family. The one missing piece is coming back.'

'I can't drop this story, Ehsaan. You know that.'

'It has serious implications, Jyoti. Let sleeping dogs lie. Look after yourself. Aryaman is coming back. You have to make a father and son reconnect emotionally. There's a lot that awaits you. Don't get into this story.'

'I will do this story, Ehsaan. You and I have come across something that needs to be brought to the forefront. I will file it tomorrow. And then, I take an indefinite break from all of this. I will recommend to the boss that you fill in for me while I'm away.'

Ehsaan closed his eyes and took a deep breath.

'You know that I want the best for you, don't you?' he said.

'I do,' Jyoti said. She put her hand on his wrist. 'It'll be fine. After tomorrow. And if you don't mind, I'm going to head home now. Spend some time with the others and approve their stories please. Fill in for me tonight. I need to talk to Aditya about his father, before he sees him tomorrow.'

Jyoti picked up her laptop bag and kept a file of documents in it. Ehsaan was watching her carefully.

'Don't worry,' she said. Something made Ehsaan feel that she was saying this to convince herself more than him.

She opened the door and walked out hurriedly. The journalists who had been waiting for her were confused by the sight of her leaving office.

'Ehsaan will go through your stories,' she told them. 'I'm sorry. Another urgent story has come up. I'll see you guys.'

She didn't wait for a response. Their questioning gazes, she felt, were burning a hole in her back as she pushed the elevator button. And she was relieved to find the elevator empty. Leaning against the metal wall, she closed her eyes and tried to make her mind stop straying and commit to one single emotion.

She stepped out of the lobby with a sense of urgency. There was work to be done. She would have to write out the last bit of the story she planned to file tomorrow. It was going to ruffle many feathers. The aftermath of the story scared her, but lives were at stake.

She tried to draw comfort from the thought of Aryaman's return. It made her feel safe again. *He will take care of it*, she said to herself. *With him by my side, nobody would be able to harm me.*

But as she stepped into her car and started the engine, the sad reality hit her. Her husband wasn't going to be the man he'd once been. The very government that he had served had crushed his spirit. How does one come back from that? How would he protect his family after having faced what he had faced?

She drove fast through the empty roads, turning up the music to help get her mind off things completely. When she heard the blare of an irritating Bollywood item song, she switched off the radio and decided to call her son. The phone rang a few times before he answered.

'Aditya,' she said. 'Make mama a pot of coffee. Don't burn yourself.'

He responded with childish exasperation. 'I know, Mum. I've done it before.'

'Also,' she said. 'I'll be home in thirty minutes. I need to speak to you. You won't be going to school tomorrow as well.'

'Wait. You want me to skip school?'

'Yes,' she said. 'It's important. Tomorrow is important . . .'

Her voice trailed away. She could feel a tear trickling down her cheek as she approached the Bandra-Worli Sea Link.

'Mum, are you okay?'

Her fourteen-year-old's words shook her. It was a simple question, but straight from the heart. In that moment, she realized what it meant to have a family more than she ever had before. Aryaman was coming back. Her son was going to love his father again. She would have someone to come home to. Or even someone to stay at home with, if possible. This was it.

'I will be, Aditya. Stay up. Wait for me.'

'Is Ehsaan uncle coming over to play PlayStation?'

Jyoti chuckled. 'Don't be a smartass. All right, see you soon. Love you.'

'Love you too, Mum.'

She sped through the Sea Link, with the windows rolled down and the breeze sweeping back her hair. The car was going well above the permitted speed limit. But she didn't care. She'd pay that damn fine for overspeeding later.

When she stopped at the next red light, Jyoti lit a cigarette. She took a deep breath and exhaled smoke. She hated herself for having developed this habit. After all, she used to scold her husband for it. But he would always say it helped take the edge off things. She now saw what he had meant. She had become a smoker over the past two years without even realizing it. She fought the urge all too often, but to no avail.

Three cigarettes later, she reached Andheri. She slowed down, searching for a vacant parking spot. Her dilapidated five-storey building was relatively small, and there weren't enough parking spots for all its tenants. She'd had to sell her Delhi house, which she had inherited from her parents, in order to be able to afford even this little place in Mumbai. Besides, with all the memories attached to the house in Delhi—of her and her father—she didn't want anything to do with that place.

She parked the car by the side of the main road, picked up her purse and exited the car.

A faint yellow glow illumined one of the windows of her flat on the top floor. Aditya was awake and had probably prepared the coffee. She would need to down all of it before she finished writing her story. And she wanted to get that done before Aryaman got home.

As she approached the entrance of the building, she wondered how she would broach the subject with Aditya. Maybe she would just break the news to him matter-of-factly. *Your father is coming back*. Or maybe she would ease into it, by explaining to her son where his father had been all these years, and why he had been there in the first place. He was an understanding fourteen-year-old, if ever there was such a thing.

Yes, she thought, *maybe that's how I will do it. Let the kid know the truth. It was time. It was time he grew up. It's a tough world out there and maybe I can't always be there to protect him.*

This was her last thought ever.

A speeding sedan rammed into her from behind and came to a screeching halt at some distance. She was thrown a few feet off the ground, landing on her skull and cracking it instantly. The contents of her purse were strewn about on the road, including the documents from the file. Death was instantaneous. The driver in the sedan, however, was not taking any chances. He reversed the car and drove over her lifeless body, just to be doubly sure.

Once he confirmed that she was dead, he stepped out of his car and retrieved the papers from the road. He took her purse as well and flung it into his car. Then, he pulled her phone out of her pocket. There was a message on the lock screen from someone called 'Arya'. It read: 'Can't wait to see you.'

The man returned to his car and drove off, leaving behind Jyoti's mangled body.

5

New Delhi

Aryaman woke up early the next morning, way before sunrise, to see his mother leaning by the hotel window and gazing outside at nothing in particular.

'Ma?'

'Go back to sleep,' Aarti said, continuing to look out. 'Don't worry about me. It's old age. I end up waking early.'

Aryaman began to sit up, reluctant to leave the comfort of the bed.

He had had a long evening the day before, spending time signing a bunch of papers at the IRW office. His mother was made to wait outside, which she did patiently. Once he was done, she took him to an expensive hotel near the airport. He told her that she didn't have to waste money on such stuff. Her playful response was that she was treating him well only for a few days, until he settled back into normal life.

Once he was in the room, he spoke to Jyoti and then sunk into the bed, dozing off like a baby. His mother lay next to him, unable to sleep all night. She just watched him sleep. And moments before he woke up, she took her seat near the window to watch the sunrise. This was part of her daily routine.

'Can I order you some coffee?' she asked him, without turning to look at him.

'That will be nice,' he replied.

She walked to the phone and called reception, ordering a pot of black coffee and a cup of tea. Then she sat beside him on the bed.

'I forgot to mention,' she said with a smile. 'We have a new addition to the family.'

Aryaman looked confused. 'I don't follow.'

'You heard me right,' she said, poker-faced. 'He is adorable. A little boy of six, I think.'

Aryaman sat upright, completely bewildered.

'But . . . How?'

Aarti shrugged. 'Found him on the streets. In Dehradun. Outside our café.'

Aryaman didn't know what to make of it. He had spent a lot of time in jail thinking about the cafeteria his mother ran. It was built on a plot owned by a retired army man, Mr Arora, and his wife. Aarti paid them a rent to stay in the little quarters behind the cafeteria. Attached to the quarters was a musty but welcoming library. Aryaman, when he wasn't on his missions, would spend hours in the library, consuming copious volumes of coffee and reading books of all kinds. Anything to take his mind off work.

Outside the library, there was a lovely garden that his mother would light up at nights with candles and lanterns. Local teenagers would come here to sing songs and strum their guitars. It was all very beautiful and innocent. And he knew why his mother had set this place up. It was to spend her twilight years living life the way she couldn't when she was younger. But this 'new addition to the family' idea was a bit much to swallow.

'Elaborate, please?' Aryaman prodded her.

'So,' she began. 'It was a long evening at the café, and I got done pretty late washing the dishes. I heard a strange noise in the back. So I picked up a knife, thinking it was a burglar . . .'

'And what? You adopted the burglar? Inducted him into the family?'

He tried to get her to spill the beans sooner, but she wasn't going to do that.

'You could say that,' she said. 'I went out and realized he was eating from the trash. Some half-eaten sandwiches and chicken bones. I tried asking him what was wrong, but he got scared and ran off with a mouthful of food. I tailed him. He was very weak, so he couldn't run fast. He finally stopped before his kid and dropped the food in front of him. The kid seemed on the verge of death, and his father was just trying to give him something to eat. But it was too late. He was too weak to eat. I saw the father weep. I decided to take him in.'

Aryaman shook his head. There was a knock on the door. Aarti asked the room attendant to place the tray on the table and thanked him before he left the room. As she poured Aryaman his coffee, she looked at his confused face.

'Well,' she said. 'I thought he was a thief, but now he's a family member. I call him Chor.'

As she said this, her face broke into a smile, and Aryaman instantly knew. He began to laugh.

'You idiot!' She laughed with him. 'You should have seen your face!'

'Ma, I thought you were against keeping animals at home!'

'Chor had lost his kid, too,' she said in a sombre tone. 'He needed someone. Unlike humans, dogs don't feel self-pity. They cry on the inside till they wither away. I found love in him; he, in me. Besides, your wife and kid love him too.'

'Is he in Mumbai with them?'

'No.' She smiled. 'He loves the cafeteria. Maybe we can go see him in the next couple of days if Jyoti is up for it.'

Aryaman drank the coffee, letting its warmth soothe his throat.

'I love Chor already,' he said. 'And I haven't even met the little chap.'

Aryaman and his mother had checked their luggage in. They were in the waiting area, sitting in silence. Neither of them knew where to start, because they had nothing to catch up on. His mother had already informed him about how wonderful Dehradun still was, how the little café offered a perfect escape from reality and how Chor filled in the emotional void that Aryaman had left behind. She also spoke fondly of her grandson, Aditya: about how he had Aryaman's eyes, how his nostrils would redden and flare up when he was angry and how he had taken after his mother in every other way. She also told Aryaman that she suspected Aditya had a girlfriend. Once, when Aditya was visiting her in Dehradun, she found him speaking to someone on his cellphone late at night. She seemed a little concerned reporting this to Aryaman, who was just amused by the whole account.

'It's their age to do such things,' he said. 'I remember I had my first cigarette when I was fourteen.'

'I knew. Just didn't know how to bring the subject up. I realized it was a passing phase and better sense would prevail eventually.'

'It did.' Aryaman smiled. 'Until I joined intelligence. And then the habit came back. Which reminds me, I desperately need a smoke now.'

As he stood up, his mother gave him a disapproving stare but chose not to chide him. Not the right time.

'Just one,' she said. 'They sell entire packs here. So you take one and give me the rest. I will help you cut back.'

Aryaman bought himself a pack from the counter outside the smoking room of the airport. He walked in and lit his cigarette, taking a seat in the corner. The room was hazy, thick with smoke. A woman was talking on the phone animatedly while puffing away. A man was reading a newspaper. A short while later, the door opened and another man walked in.

The man seemed to be taking uncertain steps, drawing closer to Aryaman, clearly wary of approaching him. He didn't have a cigarette. Aryaman took a deep drag. He saw a plane take off and get swallowed by the clouds. Then, he felt a hand on his shoulder.

It was Randheer.

Aryaman got up, nearly dropping his cigarette. None of them spoke. Aryaman didn't know how to react.

'Why are you here, Randheer?'

Randheer was silent for a long time, fighting back tears.

'I wish I had another reason to be here, Arya. But . . .'

He sounded as though he was choking on his words.

Aryaman worriedly asked, 'What?'

'Your wife,' he said, his voice trembling. 'She was murdered last night.'

6

Islamabad, Pakistan

Ashraf Asif, a senior officer of the Pakistan Intelligence Agency, stepped out of his government-issued sedan and walked into his lavish house. His driver parked the car and left the keys with his servant. After pouring himself a stiff drink, which had no real effect on him, Ashraf changed into an outfit rather unbecoming of him: hoodie, track pants and a pollution mask usually worn by asthmatics. He checked the time and then stood up. He had to be somewhere. Picking up the keys to his private vehicle, he stepped out of the house and drove off.

After he was about a kilometre away from the house, he took a sharp left turn. He looked into the rearview mirror. Then, he took another sharp turn to the left. And then one to the right. He needed to make sure nobody was tailing him. There were times he half hoped he would see someone following him, so that he could confront them and add some zest to his life. But this mission would see to that.

He pulled up outside a drab-looking building, parked right at the gate and cast one final glance over his shoulder. Having lit himself a cigarette, he walked through the entrance, which was not high enough for a man his height. He ran a hand through his sparse, grey hair as he approached the door of a flat. It seemed like any other door, but he knew that it was made of reinforced steel. He peeped through the keyhole. Not to spy on anything, but to get security clearance. Lodged into the keyhole was a device that would scan his iris before letting him into the safe house.

The door creaked open, and Ashraf went towards a large mahogany desk which had four computer screens and a bunch of wires dangling from it. He switched the computer on and placed his right thumb over a fingerprint scanner. He logged in to the system that was designed to circumvent the watchful eyes of the law, thanks to a software that intelligence agents use to access the untraceable Dark Web. Then, he opened a website that allowed him to access another special software called Scorpion. He entered the password.

Moments later, Ashraf was automatically connected to a conference call. There were no faces; only voices of seven different people could be heard. One voice belonged to the man who was the leader of this tight-knit group that called itself the Scorpion. This man, too, went by the same name—the Scorpion—and on these calls he always spoke through a voice modulator.

'Status?' his voice boomed, breaking the silence that had followed after all the members had joined the call.

'Sir,' Ashraf said. 'Biological warfare is something nobody is ever prepared for. Both the World Wars saw it. A bioweapon attack would not only cause sickness and death . . .'

'So I take it that you are confident we choose a biological attack over a straightforward explosion?'

Ashraf cleared his throat and answered, 'It causes paralysing uncertainty in a country. We will impair India in a way few have managed to.'

'And is everyone else on the same page?'

There were brief noises of approval from the rest of the committee. None of the members knew the others in this shadow organization, except for the leader, the Scorpion. Nobody knew the Scorpion, but he knew all of his agents.

'This mission is sanctioned by the Scorpion,' the leader said. 'By when will this be underway?'

'My team is in Turkey right now.' Ashraf smiled to himself. 'I have found the right people for the job. Everything's running smoothly as of now, and we should be ready to attack on the twenty-sixth.'

'Good,' the Scorpion replied. 'We'll speak soon.'

They were logged out of the system immediately after the Scorpion cut the call. Ashraf leaned back in his chair, relieved and anxious in equal measure.

Grand Bazaar, Istanbul, Turkey

The atmosphere of the Grand Bazaar, one of the world's most popular tourist attractions, was electric. As any covert operative knew, this was an ideal setting for meetings and exchanges, which were best carried out in plain sight, unless secrecy was absolutely required.

A couple negotiated their way through the labyrinthine lanes of the market, walking past rows of shops that sold furniture, carpets, jewellery and leather goods. Finally, they stopped before a shopfront that displayed an array of spices, all stocked in glass jars. The husband, bald and stocky but solid, was dressed in a Turkish kaftan and wore a tight skull cap. The wife, dressed in a simple burqa, lifted her veil to momentarily reveal her face to the shopkeeper. He noticed her hazel eyes and wheatish skin.

The husband examined the various jars on display and pointed at one that contained ground Indian saffron. The stout shopkeeper dutifully handed it out to him. After the husband was done unscrewing the jar's lid, the wife took from it a fistful of saffron, looked around to check if anyone was noticing her and slowly spilled the powdery stuff to the ground.

The shopkeeper gave her a nod and quickly got off his throne-like seat. He stepped out of the shop and walked down the street. The couple followed him through the swarm of people. They stopped outside a small store with its shutters down. The shopkeeper pulled a key out of his pocket, bent down, opened the shutters and led the couple into what seemed to be a dungeon. The husband put his hand around the wife's waist, and they both went in.

They walked through a musty, narrow space. It smelled of rotten meat and garbage. The shopkeeper approached a wooden door and knocked on it once. It opened a few seconds later, and a man—balding, bespectacled, dressed in black, built like the side of a house—stood before them with a courteous smile. A big, tough man nobody would like to mess with.

'Come in,' this man said.

Once the couple was inside, the shopkeeper went out. It was now the three of them in the stuffy room.

'Asra,' the bespectacled man said. 'Salaam.'

There was a hint of sarcasm in his tone as he continued, 'How are the husband and wife doing?'

He led them towards an upturned garbage bin with two cups of coffee placed on it.

'You can stop calling us that when it's just the three of us,' Asra Khan, a Pakistani intelligence agent working for Ashraf Asif, finally said. 'What is the update, Lior?'

Lior Meirs, of Israeli origin, was one of the world's most sought-after arms dealers. He started his career with the Mossad, but his greed had got the better of him. With years of Israeli training behind him, Lior had decided to branch out and start a business of his own. A business of war and terror nonetheless. His notoriety, as an illegal seller of weapons of mass destruction, had led to his name figuring at the top of all the intelligence watch lists around the globe.

'Using the formula you sent me,' Lior directly addressed Asra. 'I have managed to create the weapon.'

'Project Vishaanu,' scoffed the man who was playing the husband's role. 'Isn't that what the Indians called it?'

'Yeah.' Asra shrugged. 'They were up to no good as usual. But we have beaten them at their own game. They wouldn't have imagined us getting our hands on their top-secret formula.'

Lior lifted a briefcase and opened it to reveal numerous neatly placed vials filled with a viscous green liquid. The husband walked up to it and lifted a vial, examining it closely.

'Sorry, Eymen, but don't pick them up like that. If it slips and cracks, we're all in trouble,' Lior said.

Eymen, the husband, grimaced at Lior but did as he was told. Of Kurdish origin, Eymen Arsalan was an integral part of this mission against the Indian state.

He was identified by Ashraf, and when his case was presented to the Scorpion, he immediately wanted to bring Eymen on board. Eymen's hatred for Indians was unusually intense, but it was a great tool at their disposal. Lior, of course, knew nothing about the Scorpion's involvement. Or even of its existence.

'Attach it to a vest with a detonator,' Lior continued, as he packed the vials and zipped up the briefcase. 'The more the vials, the more the gas. And so, the more potent the weapon.'

'On paper it's very effective, Eymen,' Asra said, adopting a pacifying tone. 'A modified, stronger version of the Ebola virus. Anyone exposed to it will be affected within hours. And it's highly contagious. So it will spread without anyone being able to control it in time.'

Asra realized that Eymen seemed irritated. He had a lot at stake with this mission, although he never told her what his intentions were. Her boss, Ashraf Asif, and the Scorpion were the only two people who knew why Eymen had agreed to be a part of this high-risk plan.

'On paper,' Eymen said, 'I am paying a lot of money for something that has not been tested yet.' He was addressing Asra, but his aggression was directed at Lior.

'Are you questioning my work?' Lior asked with a blank expression on his face.

'I don't trust you Jews,' Eymen said, flatly.

Lior took a step towards Eymen, his fists clenched. And Eymen didn't seem intimidated at all. The tension in the room was so tangible it could be cut with a knife. Asra had to intervene; she reminded them why they were there in the first place.

She turned to Eymen first. 'Remember, we stand to lose a lot too,' she said. 'If my bosses in Islamabad deemed it worth the trouble, it has to be the real deal. They trust Lior, and we should too.'

Then she shifted her attention to Lior. 'We will wire half the money now,' she said with an air of authority. 'The remaining half after the thing has been tested.'

Lior grinned at her. When Eymen saw Lior's perfect teeth, he felt the urge to knock them in. But he needed to calm himself down. Now was not the time. Asra was his handler, and he needed to abide by her instructions.

Lior led the way till they reached a wall on which a carpet was hung. Lior pushed the carpet aside to reveal a wooden door behind it. He threw open the door and guided Eymen and Asra through a narrow passage towards an adjoining small room. When they were inside, Lior switched on the lights.

There were three dead men on the floor. The skin and flesh had melted off their bodies like wax. The ghastly sight would have made most people squirm, if not throw up. But not these people . . .

Eymen, for the first time in the last couple of hours, allowed himself a smile. Asra was impressed too.

'So Vishaanu is pretty effective.'

'The truth is before you.' Lior shrugged. 'Are you impressed yet, Eymen?'

Eymen's face straightened, but he extended his arm for a handshake and left the room feeling satisfied.

Once Eymen was out, Lior said to Asra, 'What's his deal?'

'It's personal, Lior. Leave it at that. He hasn't told me either. Just my boss at the PIA knows.'

Lior clucked his tongue. 'Well, none of my business then.'

'By the way,' Asra continued, 'two of the three have been dealt with.'

'What about the antidote?' Lior asked.

Asra shook her head.

'We'll kill her soon, though,' she said. 'Once we get what we need from her.'

On her phone, Asra showed Lior a photo of an earnest-looking woman wearing a lab coat.

'We need to do what we need to do,' Lior said with a sad smile. 'Though it's a pity. She's a pretty woman, this Dr Avantika Advani.'

7

Their wedding was an intimate event. Just the people who mattered to Aryaman and Jyoti had been invited to a rather upscale hotel in one of New Delhi's posher localities.

Since socializing didn't come naturally to Aryaman, he struggled to smile throughout the evening as he thanked his few guests. None of Aryaman's colleagues attended the wedding, even though they wanted to. In his line of work, one avoided social gatherings. Everyone had to keep their professional life secret and their private lives separate. Mixing the two messed up the equation.

At one point in the evening, Jyoti excused herself to freshen up.

'I need to talk to you,' Aryaman said, following her into the ladies' room.

'Can't it wait?' she said, a little taken aback upon seeing him walk in like this.

She noticed that he looked strikingly handsome.

'Aren't you having second thoughts?' he asked.

The colour began to drain from Jyoti's face as she said, 'Don't do this to me, Aryaman. Not today.'

'No,' he said, taking a step towards her. 'Marrying a person like me is not going to be easy. I will always love you before everything else. But just the way I'm wired, sometimes, I'll have to make a decision when the country will come first.'

His voice had dimmed. She could sense the struggle it had cost him to say all this.

'Aryaman.' She smiled gently. 'It's what I have chosen.'

'And if I die in the line of duty?'

Tears welled up in her eyes. 'That won't happen.'

'There's a strong possibility it will,' he said matter-of-factly, as he wiped a tear that trickled down her face.

The door to the washroom opened. An elderly lady was about to step in when she saw the two of them and froze awkwardly.

'Aunty.' Aryaman smiled at her. 'Two minutes, please. Some life decisions being made here.'

The lady entered anyway and hobbled towards one of the booths.

'Don't let me disturb you,' she smiled and said, locking the door from inside the booth.

Aryaman turned towards Jyoti and looked into her eyes.

'You're not going anywhere, Aryaman. Death will probably take me first,' she said half-jokingly, to ease the tension.

'Bullshit,' he said as he held her in a tight embrace. 'That's never going to happen.' He kissed her on the forehead. 'We're going to die natural deaths.' He smiled. 'That's the best thing that can happen to us.'

'That's the most romantic thing you've said all evening.' She chuckled.

Aryaman turned around to leave, but Jyoti tugged at his arm. He regarded her confusedly. She pointed at one of the unoccupied booths and winked.

'Really? These damn clothes will take an hour to get out of,' he whispered, so the elderly lady wouldn't hear.

Jyoti pulled him into the booth and locked the door. The lady stepped out of her booth and looked at the door that had just been shut. She sighed and mumbled something about kids these days having no decency.

Aryaman felt his insides tighten as he saw, one last time for the night, Jyoti's naked, mangled body on a cold, stone slab at the morgue. His mother, his son and Randheer were waiting for him outside. He had been alone with her for over an hour before his mother entered the room to take him away. She avoided looking at Jyoti's body; she knew she wouldn't have the strength to survive that blow. Seeing Aryaman had shaken her up enough.

Tears streamed down Aryaman's face as the attendant led him to Jyoti's body and lifted the pristine white sheets. The man left soon after. Aryaman pressed his forehead against hers and closed his eyes. Her face was wet with his tears.

He saw her brutally destroyed body. Her skin was pale, dappled with patches of purple and red. He felt her crushed bones under his fingers. He turned around, let out a yell and punched the wall. Then he dropped to the ground.

'I'm sorry, baby. I'm sorry.'

He walked out of the morgue emptier than when he had entered. Fate, clearly, wasn't done with him.

Aditya hadn't seen his mother's body in the gruesome state that his father had, but the trauma wasn't any easier for him to bear. He watched the woman who had given him life burn away on the pyre. The sight of his father's shaky hands lighting the logs of wood had hit him in the gut.

At the funeral, Aryaman noticed Randheer talking animatedly with Jyoti's colleague Ehsaan. He was too numb to speak to them, so he walked back to his son and held him by the shoulders.

'Your mother never told you what I did in the past, Aditya. You know me as a man with a drinking problem. A bad father. A bad husband. A waste of space even. But I wasn't so, once upon a time. And I swear, I will not spare the people who did this.'

Aditya had nothing to say. He just nodded, so his father would stop speaking. He walked away and stood next to his grandmother. This little act of his stung Aryaman in a way he couldn't have imagined.

The Hindu priest performed Jyoti's last rites. Most people had paid their respects and had left. Eventually, what remained was the burning pyre—its flickering flames—with Aryaman, his family and Randheer standing near it, as the priest and his assistants began to clean up the area.

Aryaman walked towards his mother. He leaned over to speak into her ear, so Aditya wouldn't hear him.

'Take him and wait in the car. I will settle the money with the priest. And I need to have a word with Randheer.'

Soon after, she led a listless Aditya away.

Aryaman turned to approach Randheer, who was already striding towards him.

'Randheer,' Aryaman said tiredly. 'This. This won't go down well for you. Leave if you have to.'

'I am going nowhere, Arya. Definitely not now.'

Aryaman was about to speak when Randheer lifted his hand to stop him. He gave Aryaman a cell phone. There was a video on it, waiting to be played: the footage of the assassin getting into a car and zipping off. He was a rather large man.

'No face. Nothing,' Randheer said. 'Just a video of him getting into his car. He's a big son of a bitch.'

Aryaman sighed and handed Randheer his phone back.

'I will figure this out, Randheer. Thanks for trying . . .'

'Let me complete,' Randheer said. 'I ran the number plates. They're bogus. But . . . I have fed it into our Gait Identification System.'

'And?' Aryaman lit himself a cigarette, watching the pyre.

'It matched that of a certain Lars Christiansen,' Randheer said. 'European hitman. Works for hire, so his motive would have been nothing more than money.'

This took Aryaman by surprise. 'Is he still in town?'

Randheer nodded and showed Aryaman a video analysis of Lars's gait.

'We don't have the means to run this ourselves, Aryaman. Local agencies will take over.'

Aryaman blew out a cloud of smoke.

'Fuck them. She was my wife.'

'And she had information that these bastards didn't want leaked out. I spoke to her friend, who'd asked her to drop the story.'

Aryaman processed this information silently. He had suspected this when he'd seen the two of them talking.

'What story was this?'

'Wouldn't say. Wanted me to show my badge. We can get into trouble for taking matters in our own hands . . . Grant me some credit, Aryaman. I have been reduced to a desk agent, but my mind is still sharp. I knew I had to break the news to you.'

Aryaman took one long, last drag of his cigarette and threw it on the ground, crushing it under his shoe.

'Where is Christiansen?'

Goa, a few hours later . . .

Aryaman and Randheer exited the airport and got into the car that the latter had arranged. During the flight, Randheer had told Aryaman all he knew and showed him, on an iPad, the few file photos that the internal IRW directory had of Lars Christiansen, who was in India under a fake name: Lucas Hansen.

Randheer also mentioned that Christiansen worked as a bodyguard for a private security firm, which assigned its men to top European celebrities who toured around the world. In fact, that very night, Christiansen was handling the security detail for a

Swedish DJ slated to perform on an upscale cruise ship, which even had an in-house casino.

'Funny thing is, Christiansen came to Mumbai a month prior to this DJ's arrival,' Randheer said as they drove towards Panjim. 'Something doesn't feel right about why he killed Jyoti the way he did. It was rather shabby for someone with his skills.'

'Shabby? She was my fucking wife,' Aryaman spat out before he lighting another cigarette.

'Aryaman?'

'Randheer, just fucking drive.'

'Maybe you're right,' Randheer said. 'This is a terrible idea. We should turn back and let the law take care of this.'

Aryaman glared at him. Then he spoke in a voice bereft of emotion. 'The hit was probably decided last minute, in my opinion. Jyoti was never supposed to die in their initial plan. Whoever "they" are.'

Randheer watched Aryaman's cigarette burn out and the ash drop on his shirt.

'Randheer, you can drop me at that damn casino and get back to work on the first flight out of here. But I'm going to end the son of a bitch who did this to my wife.'

The rest of the drive passed in silence. Aryaman looked ahead at the dark highway as they sped towards the location where Christiansen and the DJ were supposed to be.

They pulled up not far from where the lavishly decorated cruise ship was docked. A narrow wooden path led to the ship, which was fitted with a staircase to climb aboard. Aryaman scanned for the various entry and exit points. There seemed just one way to enter and exit, since the ship was already afloat. Stepping out of the car, Randheer handed Aryaman a ticket to the DJ's event.

Randheer began to put on a dinner jacket as they approached the entrance. Aryaman gripped Randheer's hand and, eyeing the jacket, said, 'It will look better on me.'

'Well, I'm sorry but you might have to get your own.'

But Aryaman, much to Randheer's surprise, wasn't joking. 'I don't think you're needed. Just track me. I will be on the phone with you throughout and update you as I go along.'

'No offence,' Randheer said, 'but he can snap you like a twig.'

'Let me worry about that,' Aryaman said as he pointed at the ship. 'There's just this one route to enter and exit the ship. By the time I'm done with Christiansen, I don't think getting away from this route will be an option.'

Aryaman saw the few motorboats hitched at the pier. Randheer followed Aryaman's gaze and then, looking back at Aryaman, got the hint. He tore his ticket dramatically. Aryaman put on the jacket. It didn't do him justice but masked the shabbiness of his crumpled shirt and jeans.

'These were expensive, just so you know.'

Aryaman allowed himself a smile as he firmly held Randheer's shoulders.

'If I come out alive, I'll refund the amount.'

'Trust me,' Randheer implored. 'I'm ready for this.'

Aryaman boarded the ship and, showing his ticket at the security counter, headed straight for the casino. Randheer watched him walk past the tough bouncers as they frisked him for weapons. They found none, of course. *Aryaman is the weapon,* Randheer thought.

Randheer had his work cut out. Three motorboats were chained to the pier. A guard sat comfortably on the landing, earphones plugged in. He probably had the keys to unlock the boats. But first, Randheer had to park the car at the next dock, so that they could make a quick getaway after the mission.

But Aryaman had no plans on how to accomplish this mission yet. The thought didn't worry Randheer as much as the reality of Aryaman going in did. He was on that ship unarmed, rusty and still reeling emotionally from a hole in his heart.

Aryaman was transported into an entirely different world on the ship. The casino, though grand in appearance, had all kinds of crass people gambling their ill-gotten money away. Aryaman had never seen the inside of a casino. *Well, these motherfuckers haven't seen the inside of the kind of prison I have,* Aryaman thought sourly.

With his head hanging low to avoid the CCTVs capturing his face, Aryaman made his way towards the third level of the ship, where the DJ, apparently called Wesley, was performing. He entered through a narrow corridor that led to the suites and smaller rooms. The casino below was pleasant in comparison to the disco-like hall where the DJ was performing. The stench of alcohol and smoke enveloped everything.

Aryaman's face contorted in disgust as the jarring electronic dance music blared from the speakers. He pushed past a few twenty-somethings who were dancing wildly in their drunken stupor. As he got to the front, he got a clear view of the peroxide-blonde DJ who was hopping and stupidly waving his arms to match the beat. Aryaman scanned the guards behind the DJ. Two Indians, and Lars Christiansen. *Jyoti's killer . . .*

Unfazed by the noise, Christiansen stood with his arms crossed, carefully surveying the crowd. Aryaman felt his rage boiling over. He walked across to the bar and ordered a vodka, neat. He lit a cigarette, took the glass and walked towards Wesley.

He waited for a set to end before yelling out, 'Hey, motherfucker! Yes you, you piece of shit. Wesley. Play some real music!' He sounded adequately drunk

Wesley looked at Aryaman, shrugged and laughed. He played his next track. Aryaman continued to sway,

playing the part of a sloshed man. The stone-faced
Christiansen had his eyes on him. Aryaman showed him
the middle-finger and laughed, but Christiansen didn't
react. Then, Aryaman made his move. He filled his
mouth with vodka, ran towards the DJ console, spat it
all out on Wesley's face and started laughing maniacally.
Wesley was stunned. A few people, who had noticed
this, were laughing. The others were too immersed in
the music to care. Christiansen sprang into action and
dragged Aryaman out through the backdoor.

'I'll handle this bastard,' Christiansen said to the
two guards who were part of the security detail. 'Keep
an eye on the boss. Get him a towel to wipe his face.'

They were in another corridor, almost mirroring
the one that Aryaman had entered the venue through.
Christiansen's grip around Aryaman's nape was firm.
He was dragged into a room and then slammed against
the wall by Christiansen. But Aryaman looked back at
him defiantly, long and hard; he was face to face with
his wife's killer. He felt a rage he hadn't felt in years
as he observed Christiansen's pale, rough face and his
cold, blue eyes.

'It's best you leave now, mister.'

Aryaman's face hardened. He shook with the anger
that was building up within him.

'Do we have a problem, dude?'

'I was hoping you'd ask, Lucas. Or should I say . . .
Lars Christiansen?'

Christiansen's eyes widened.

'I've never met a man,' Aryaman continued, 'who wouldn't have a problem with his wife getting killed.'

Christiansen swiftly reached for his gun and pressed it into Aryaman's belly. Smiling, Aryaman looked up at the CCTV camera.

'Why did you do it?' Aryaman said. 'Or maybe you can tell me in private. I'm sure your DJ boss does drugs in that suite there which doesn't have CCTVs. Am I right?'

Christiansen dragged Aryaman to Wesley's suite, opening the door with his electronic card. He shoved Aryaman towards a wall, still aiming his gun at him. Aryaman raised his hands.

'Who the fuck are you?' Christiansen asked him.

Aryaman noticed Christiansen's tense stance and bulging muscles.

'Have the steroids damaged your brains, Christiansen? Why did you kill my wife? I know you're a contract killer. Just tell me who ordered the hit and I might make this less painful for you.'

Christiansen smirked as he made his way to the corner of the grand suite. He pulled out a silencer from a drawer and screwed it on to his gun.

'You're a loose end,' he said softly. 'Guess I've got to tie you up.'

'Do you really need a silencer with all that noise your boss is making outside?'

Aryaman scanned the room out of the corner of his eye. He saw an unopened bottle of champagne in an ice bucket; a small glass table with a few lines of cocaine and a laptop on it; a pool table slightly away from him. Aryaman calculated his moves in his head.

Christiansen raised the gun and was about to shoot when Aryaman leapt across to the pool table, picked up the champagne bottle and flung it at Christiansen, who got startled but moved aside in the nick of time and fired a volley of bullets. Aryaman took cover behind the pool table. He picked up the balls on the table and threw them with great force at Christiansen, sending him diving for cover behind a sofa. The 8 ball smashed into Christiansen's nose and split it open.

Aryaman charged at him. Both the men matched each other's moves, each landing the occasional blow. But Christiansen soon overpowered Aryaman and began pounding him repeatedly with his fist. Bruised and winded, Aryaman struggled to catch his breath.

The moment Christiansen eased up with the punches, Aryaman kicked him in the crotch and broke free of his grip. He then picked up the laptop and whacked it against Christiansen's head, disorienting him for a second. Aryaman then saw his chance. He wrenched the gun out of Christiansen's hand and shot him in the kneecap.

'Why did you kill my wife?' he screamed.

'The bitch probably had it coming.'

Aryaman shot him in the other kneecap. Christiansen was now yelping in pain.

'I will die before I say a word.'

Christiansen slipped a hand into his pocket and began to fiddle with something. The next instant, Aryaman seized his arm and wrenched out of his hand the phone he had been trying to use. Its display flashed this message: 'Restoring to factory settings.' Aryaman aborted the command just in time. Christiansen mustered the strength to throw one final blow at Aryaman, who evaded it comfortably. Using a jagged piece of porcelain from a broken plate, Aryaman stabbed Christiansen in the throat. The blood spurted out.

'Have it your way then.'

The music outside had died down. There were a few rounds of knocks on the door. Aryaman presumed it was either Wesley, or the guards wanting to check on Christiansen. Either way, he needed to get out of the suite. He looked at the glass window and pulled out his own phone. Randheer was on the line.

'Third level,' Aryaman said. 'I'm going to get into the sea.'

'I've got the boat,' came the reply from Randheer. 'Ready when you are.'

Aryaman pocketed Christiansen's gun and then lifted his lifeless, heavy body. With great force he rammed the body into the glass window, smashing it open. First, he threw Christiansen's body out. Then, just as the door behind him was kicked open, he jumped out himself, landing hard on the water.

Randheer sped towards Aryaman and helped him on to the boat. The guards began to fire at them from above while calling for backup. Dodging the bullets with much difficulty, Randheer steered the boat away.

'Why did he do it?'

'Wouldn't say,' Aryaman responded, weakly. 'There's honour among thieves clearly.'

'He tried to erase the data in his phone,' Aryaman continued, pulling out the drenched phone and handing it to Randheer. 'I managed to stop him. I'm sure there's something important on it. Extract the data as soon as you can.'

They sped towards the shore, and the boat soon came to a halt. Randheer examined the phone, wiping it dry and then dismantling it to stop the water from seeping into the hardware.

'We'll clean up and get back to Mumbai tonight itself. The Goan authorities will be after us in no time. I had to thrash a security guard to get this boat.'

But Aryaman wasn't listening. He had blacked out on the floor of the boat, blood and water mingling around his body.

'And he thinks he's ready for this,' Randheer sighed.

8

Islamabad, Pakistan

Ashraf Asif was not sure how the Scorpion would take the latest piece of news. He took the usual precautions to shake off any tail and reached the secret location to phone his boss. The Scorpion didn't usually encourage one-to-one calls. But Ashraf wanted his core team to be aware of all aspects of the operations. He sent out a distress signal to indicate that he had something important to report. And the Scorpion, a paranoid man in many ways, responded almost immediately by setting up a time to chat with him.

When Ashraf logged in to the software through the Dark Web, he found the Scorpion was already waiting online. Ashraf had been all of forty seconds late in joining in.

'Sir,' he said urgently. 'The bioweapon has been picked up by my people. You will also be glad to know that the journalist who was nosing into our affairs has been taken care of.'

Ashraf lit a cigarette and rubbed his temple nervously.

'Then why did you set up this call? This seems like good news.'

'Sir,' Ashraf continued, mustering up the courage to deliver the news. 'The hitman who took care of the journalist was killed soon after. In Goa, while he was undercover. We don't know who did it.'

There was silence at the other end. Ashraf waited for a bit, hoping the Scorpion would say something.

'That isn't all,' Ashraf resumed, his voice struggling to maintain its composure. 'The scientist who has the antidote to the bioweapon that Lior Myers created is on the run. Her name is Dr Avantika Advani. My people should find her soon and take care of it. That won't be a problem, but it is something you should know.'

The Scorpion didn't speak.

'Sir?' Ashraf prompted him for a response.

'Okay. Find out who killed your hitman. And get the antidote to the bioweapon. Without that, even we are susceptible to its effects.'

Ashraf had expected a strict rebuke and was relieved by what he heard.

'Yes, sir. We are working on this.'

'Good,' the Scorpion said flatly. 'Or you would have failed at your assignment. And you know how much I hate that.'

Ashraf did know. He'd heard stories he didn't want to think about right now. The phone went dead. The cigarette had burnt out to a stub in his hand without him realizing.

IRW office, Mumbai

Randheer was not way out of line in entering the IRW's Mumbai office. But he wasn't exactly welcome either. The station chief, Rajendra Nath, was a little surprised to find that he had a visitor from New Delhi. Nath, who reported directly to Bipin Sharma, was touted as the next in line after Sharma's promotion to Ashish Singh's position.

Nath had walked in a little late that morning and had seen Randheer sitting with a young techie. Randheer, too, had noticed Nath but chose to pretend otherwise. When Nath drew closer and it became absolutely impossible to ignore him, Randheer feigned obedience and respectfully offered a greeting.

'Give us a minute, please.' Nath snapped his fingers at the techie, who scurried away, leaving Randheer and

Nath looking at each other. A tired, polite smile on Randheer's face, and a scowl on Nath's.

'Randheer . . . Didn't know you were coming. What has Delhi got you into this time? You didn't care to inform me in advance?'

Inform me in advance, Randheer repeated the words in his head. *Motherfucking bureaucrats want to be informed about everything in advance, as if they are in the business of selling groceries. The 26/11 attackers didn't inform you in advance, you bastard. Neither did those responsible for the '93 blasts. Maybe you should send your terrorist friends a memo requesting that they mail you before they plan to fuck your country up.*

'Now will you tell me why you are here?'

Randheer's internal monologue had left him staring blankly at Nath. He simply picked up a copy of that morning's newspaper, already opened to the right page, and held it up for Nath to read: MAYHEM IN GOA CASINO.

Randheer's voice dropped to a whisper. 'Delhi didn't send me, sir. I'm investigating a lead.'

'Lead? What case?' Nath folded his arms, trying to appear intimidating.

'Can't say now but it could be something, sir. I'm just letting you know that I currently have unimpeded access to the IRW units across the country, if need be.'

Randheer's words were meant to annoy Nath. He knew what was coming, and he was prepared for it.

'And you choose to do it on my watch?' Nath asked. 'Why aren't you using the tech team back in Delhi?'

'I don't have answers to all questions yet, sir. But I wouldn't be here if there was no threat.'

Nath took the newspaper from Randheer and scanned the article.

'An international hitman. Killed in Goa last night. But I knew this yesterday itself.'

Ignoring Nath's blatant lie, Randheer said, 'I've got the hitman's phone. We're figuring out his next target.'

'You were in Goa? Are you responsible for his death?'

Nath's queries were met with silence.

'Sir, I can't talk about it,' Randheer said with a smile. 'And if you ask the bosses back in New Delhi, I don't think they can either. Not at the moment.'

Randheer had worded his sentence carefully, to make Nath think that Bipin Sharma was involved. The fear of his boss, Randheer hoped, would stop Nath from digging around.

In parting, Randheer decided to soften the blow with a dose of respect. 'I will tell you everything. I promise. Just give me some time.'

'Don't take too long,' Nath said.

Randheer went back to the computer where Christiansen's phone was plugged in. He looked at the progress bar on the software. Just a few more minutes and he would have complete access to the phone's contents. Aryaman was relying on him. *I hope he gets his answers soon,* Randheer thought.

9

Aryaman watched his son, who stood at the window, gazing down at the bustling streets of south Mumbai. They had rented a small flat here, as Aryaman's instinct told him that going back to Jyoti's house immediately wasn't a wise move. Maybe they were being watched. Maybe this was connected to his release from prison. It didn't add up, but he didn't want to take any chances.

His mother was in the kitchen, making omelettes. He went there to help her, after his son had thwarted several of his attempts at making conversation.

'Is he still not responding to you?' Aarti asked him, adding chopped onions and chillies into the sizzling pan.

He walked up to her, wiped the beads of sweat off her forehead with the back of his hand, and stared unseeingly at the pan.

'I had plans of putting together all the broken pieces I had left behind,' he said, his voice quivering.

'But fate isn't done with me. It's taken those broken pieces and shattered them into smaller, sharper shards. I don't think I can come back from this, Ma.'

He broke down. His mother watched him as tears streamed down his face. She resisted the urge to console him. *Nothing can make this better for him,* she thought. *I should just let it pass. He was trained for these things. He is going to bounce back and I will be by his side, of course. But my words and hugs aren't going to heal him. Seeing this through to the end will.*

She scraped the omelette off the pan and placed it on a plate. She handed it to him and pointed at the room where her grandson was. Aryaman wiped his face, picked up the plate and trudged towards his son. He placed the plate before Aditya and waited for his reaction. There was none. Aryaman leaned against the window and lit a cigarette. Down on the street, passers-by went about their lives.

He longed for Aditya to say something to him. To cry. To curse him for not being there. Anything. But the boy's stoic silence disturbed him. Aryaman attempted to talk again, 'You're allowed to cry, you know.'

Aditya turned to face his father. Although his mother had told him otherwise, Aryaman saw more of his own reflection in Aditya than Jyoti's.

'Mom used to say I'm like a volcano,' Aditya said. 'Silent. Holding in all that it should let out. Until it does.'

Aryaman kept quiet, observing his boy's tone, the quiet strength that it held.

'She used to say I'm like you,' Aditya continued, looking at his father blow out a cloud of smoke.

Aryaman, despite himself, smiled ever so slightly at this.

'Don't smile like it's a compliment.'

Aryaman's face straightened obediently. His son was finally opening up.

'Did your mother tell you what I did for a living?'

Aditya shrugged. 'She said she'd tell me when I grow up. Guess you are going to have to tell me yourself . . . *Dad*?'

Aryaman felt his heartbeat quicken. *Dad*. He didn't know when he had last heard his son call him that.

'She did say you are some kind of cop, though. But a cop without the uniform.'

Aryaman nodded. 'That is one way to put it.'

Aditya reached out for Aryaman's bruised cheek—an injury from his face-off with Christiansen—and ran his finger over the clotted blood.

'I fell,' Aryaman attempted to explain.

'Bullshit,' Aditya smirked. 'Even I wouldn't use that excuse, Dad. Mum always said that keeping the truth from someone is better than lying to them.'

Well, that's what I always told your mum, Aryaman thought.

'Dad,' he said. 'Will you find the people who did this to Mum?'

'I won't rest until I do. I will find them and I will finish them. I loved your mother a lot, Aditya. And I love you a lot too.'

'Then why did you leave?'

Aryaman gave Aditya a large morsel of the omelette and ran a hand through his son's hair.

'You know what a spy does, Aditya?'

'Of course,' Aditya replied through the mouthful of food. 'They wear suits and kill the bad guys. I have a couple of spy games on my PlayStation.'

Aryaman let out a chuckle. 'Of course. That's exactly it. But not all of them wear suits . . .'

The ring of the doorbell interrupted their conversation. It was Randheer, walking towards them with a sense of urgency.

'Uncle,' Adtiya asked Randheer, still chewing on the same morsel. 'Are you a spy too? How do you know Dad?'

Randheer looked confusedly at the kid and handed over an iPad to Aryaman, who quickly began to swipe through the intel Randheer had gathered from Christiansen's phone. There were pictures of the people that Lars had killed—two middle-aged men and Jyoti—along with their personal information. He clicked on Jyoti's profile, which had the following line added to it: 'Belongings were retrieved and destroyed as ordered. Target eliminated.'

A *target*. That's what they had reduced his wife to. A wave of rage swept over Aryaman. 'This doesn't give us much,' he said.

'Check the next slide,' Randheer said. Aryaman squinted at the iPad, a little confused about how to switch between applications. Randheer leaned over and did it for him. 'His next target.'

The photo showed a woman, presumably in her thirties, wearing a lab coat. It was captioned, Dr Avantika Advani.

'Good. So we will save her life.'

'I can't figure it out yet,' Randheer said. 'But there's a clear connection between all these people. Jyoti included. I have asked a few trusted members of my team to run a background check.'

Aditya had finished the omelette by now. He managed to catch a glimpse of the iPad when Aryaman placed it on the table. Aditya picked up the iPad and stared at Dr Avantika Advani's photo.

'I have seen this lady before. Mum had pictures of her.'

Both Aryaman and Randheer looked at him expectantly. Randheer showed him the rest of the photos as well.

'Yes, Mum had pictures of these two men and the lady.'

Aryaman grasped Aditya's hand and kneeled before him.

'Did Mum ever meet them?'

'I don't know.' Aditya shrugged. 'But she had their pictures, for sure. Ehsaan Uncle from her office will know. Both of them were looking at the photos together one night.'

Aryaman got to his feet as Randheer said to him, 'Guess Ehsaan Uncle didn't tell us something we needed to know.'

'Let's pay him a visit then,' Aryaman said.

The drive to Jyoti's office was excruciatingly long. Aryaman smoked throughout the trip, lost in thought. Randheer was at the wheel, navigating the jammed streets. Aryaman had insisted on taking along Aditya, who sat in the back, his earphones on and eyes closed.

'I think he should go with your mother to Dehradun,' Randheer said. 'At least until all of this goes away.'

'And if it doesn't go away anytime soon?'

Randheer had no answer.

Aryaman sighed. 'The sooner he rids himself of his naivety, the better. The world is garbage, so let's not sugarcoat shit for him.' He turned to look at his son, who had fallen fast asleep.

Randheer's phone began to ring. He held it to his ear with one shoulder and carefully listened to what he was being told, making brief murmurs of acknowledgment. Finally, he disconnected the call and turned to Aryaman.

'So, the two deceased men were both scientists. The lady, too. Working on a classified government project.'

'Classified? Find out more.'

'Can't. Above my pay grade. I'll get crucified for poking around this.'

Aryaman knew that Randheer was already doing enough for him. 'What about the lady? Avantika Advani? Do we know where she could be?' he asked.

Randheer shook his head in frustration. 'Not yet. Her number is defunct. Our system could find no other details that will help us get in touch with her.'

Aryaman ran his hand through his hair and slammed the dashboard. 'Jyoti,' he said under his breath. 'What the hell did you get yourself into?'

The car pulled up outside Jyoti's office. Aryaman gently patted his son's head to wake him up. 'Come on, Aditya. We're going to find out what happened to Mum.'

Led by a security guard, they made their way through the busy newsroom to Ehsaan's cabin.

Ehsaan wore the look of a man who wasn't expecting any guests, but when he saw the three of them, he nodded at the guard, who left the cabin right away.

Randheer did most of the talking initially. Aryaman could tell through Ehsaan's body language that he was scared and still traumatized by the memory of Jyoti's death. Randheer told Ehsaan about the two scientists and showed him their photos on the iPad. Ehsaan didn't seem surprised.

Aryaman picked up the day's edition and read one of the headlines: Jyoti Khanna and Her Undying Quest for the Truth. The story was accompanied by a picture of Jyoti smiling ear to ear, and it carried Ehsaan's byline. Aditya took the paper from Aryaman's hand. Perching himself on a side table, he began to read the article about his mother.

'I don't want to end up like them,' Ehsaan said in a shaky voice. 'They'll kill me too.'

'Who?' Randheer pressed him for an answer.

Aryaman leaned towards Ehsaan. 'Nobody will touch you. You have my word on that. Do this for Jyoti and her son. If not for me . . . She was your best friend, wasn't she?'

Ehsaan's eyes welled up. He had a gentle face, almost cherubic, but lined with wrinkles that had no business being there this early. Aryaman placed a hand on his shoulder reassuringly.

'You have my word. Whoever they are, I won't let them harm you.'

Ehsaan took a gulp of water and then looked at Aditya.

'Can we ask him to wait in his mother's cabin?'

Aditya was watching them intently.

'He stays,' Aryaman said. 'He has the right to know what happened to his mother.'

Ehsaan unlocked a drawer and pulled out a newspaper clipping that carried the photo of one of the deceased scientists. The name 'Sunil Padmanabhan' was printed below. The article had been written by Jyoti.

10

'It all started with a mysterious call,' Ehsaan said, leaning forward on his chair, his fingers interlocked. 'Jyoti had agreed to meet the caller. She asked me to come along with her and wait some distance away. If things went south, I would be there to call the cops.'

Aryaman lit a cigarette inside the air-conditioned cabin, Ehsaan's disapproving look doing nothing to deter him.

'I saw Jyoti pacing around the promenade before she was finally asked to sit next to an odd-seeming couple,' Ehsaan continued. 'She sat slightly away from them but within earshot. They were, as I learnt later, Rajat Mehta and Avantika Advani, whose photos you showed me.'

Ehsaan pointed at Rajat's photo: a huge guy with a roundish face and a disproportionately big nose.

'What did they tell Jyoti?'

'They talked about another of their scientist friends, Sunil. They said that they were the three civilian scientists hired covertly by the government to develop a virus that could potentially be used as a bioweapon. They were to work out of a secret military premises in Navi Mumbai. The project was titled Operation Vishaanu. And it had been underway for the past six years. They said it could be the most potent bioweapon ever developed.'

'And Sunil was the first guy to be killed?' Randheer asked.

'Yes,' Ehsaan said. 'A "biohacker", as they called him. Someone who could play around with gene compositions and manipulate DNA to create a completely new organism. He's the one whose death Jyoti was investigating.'

Aryaman's attention shifted to Aditya, who had been listening intently.

'Go on,' Randheer said.

Ehsaan pulled out another file from his drawer.

'Jyoti didn't believe it at first,' Ehsaan said with a shake of his head. 'But they gave her a classified folder. They told her it's just one of many such folders. It had information about Operation Vishaanu. She shook hands with them and came back to me in the car. We were stunned to see the file.'

Aryaman took the file and browsed through it. He then handed it to Randheer, who gave it a cursory look. This was way more intricate than they had imagined.

'Continue,' Aryaman said to Ehsaan.

'We spent all night studying the documents. The scientists were working on a weaponized strain of the Ebola virus. The instructions on how to make it had been redacted. But it was authentic. Sunil and Rajat had finally developed the virus prototype, and it was supposed to be tested soon. Avantika was in charge of developing the antidote, but her prototype was not ready yet. After Sunil's "suicide", they feared that the details of the virus were going to fall into the wrong hands.'

Aryaman scratched his chin. Jyoti's death seemed to have opened up a Pandora's box. And it looked like he was the one who would have to put the lid on it as he went about avenging his wife's death.

'According to what those two told Jyoti, Sunil had hooked up with a woman about a month before. Some girl he met on Facebook. And then a few days before he died, she put him on to someone, asking him to sell the formula of the prototype for a ludicrous amount. He refused. He had realized that the lady was a spy. He didn't have a picture or anything of her. Her Facebook profile and social media presence had been wiped clean off the net. The next thing you know, he's dead. And the formula, in all probability, was taken from his personal safe.'

'The classic case of a honeytrap,' Randheer scoffed. 'Men can never hold it in their pants.'

Aryaman shot him a reproving look and then turned to see if Aditya had understood Randheer's remark. It seemed like he had.

'Oh, what?' Randheer asked. 'Murder and bioterrorism can be discussed before him but not sex?'

'Just continue,' Aryaman resignedly said to Ehsaan.

'Jyoti and I were working all night at her place when Avantika reached out to her in a rather odd way,' he said. 'Jyoti received a password and a link on her phone. When she logged in, she found herself on the Dark Web. It was a gaming chat room, where illegal money was being gambled on. But apparently the chat service was pretty secure, and that's how Jyoti and Avantika were to communicate with each other.'

Ehsaan took a quick gulp of water. 'What Avantika told Jyoti shook both of us to the core. The message read: "Rajat is dead. They got him too." When we didn't respond to the text, Jyoti's phone started buzzing with an incoming call from a strange number. It was Avantika, masking her number. She begged Jyoti for help. She told her that Rajat hadn't been answering his phone, and that she drove down to his house and found cops waiting there.'

'And he was found dead, too? "Suicide" again?' Randheer said.

'Something like that,' Ehsaan said. 'Apparently, he'd had a drink too many and toppled over from his balcony. Avantika felt the cops were in on it. She told her that going to the government would mean exposing herself to a mole, in case there was any in the system. And that would mean she could get bumped off. Since the whole project was a secret . . .'

Aryaman lit another cigarette and closed his eyes, letting the information sink in.

'On the night she got killed, Jyoti was about to file the story on Operation Vishaanu and the two dead scientists,' Ehsaan said remorsefully. 'I was trying to convince her against it. I didn't want her risking her life. But she wanted to save Avantika from meeting the same fate her colleagues had met. And doing the story was the only way she thought she could do that.'

'Had I been there earlier, this would not have happened,' Aryaman said.

A strange silence enveloped the room. It was Aditya who broke it.

'It's not your fault, Dad. Mum would have gone ahead with the story anyway, and they would have got to her one way or the other.'

Ehsaan pointed at the file on his table. 'She had the same file on her when she left office,' he said. 'My guess is, it was taken from her after she was killed. But the killer didn't realize I have a copy too. She kept me out of the picture, and that's why they came only for her.'

'Do you think Avantika is alive?'

Ehsaan appeared stressed out, with beads of sweat glistening on his forehead.

'On the last page of the file I have scribbled down a code that can help you log in to the gaming chat room through the Dark Web. I haven't dared to find out, but if Avantika is alive, maybe you can try reaching out to her through this.'

Aryaman stood up, and Randheer and Aditya followed suit.

'Thank you for being there for my wife,' Aryaman said to Ehsaan with a firm handshake and walked out of the cabin without waiting for his response.

'I will get you some security,' Randheer reassured Ehsaan and wrote down his number on a piece of paper. 'Plain-clothed officers, who you will never see, will guard you. Anything else comes to mind, just call. Thanks for the help.'

Before leaving, Aditya gave Ehsaan a hug. 'Dad will take care of the men who did this, Ehsaan Uncle. He promised me.'

As they drove back home, Aryaman began to join the dots.

'So I guess Avantika has the formula to the antidote,' he said. 'They need it before they use the weapon. To safeguard themselves from the outbreak. And these guys, whoever they are, won't rest until they get that from her.'

Randheer agreed. 'This needs to go to the higher-ups. They can find out who is orchestrating all of this. And what they plan to do with that weapon, Vishaanu.'

'Not before we reach out to Avantika,' Aryaman said. 'She's in immediate danger. And you can tell the officials what you must after that. An insider might also kill her.'

Randheer paused and thought about all the possible ways this could play out. One thing was certain, they didn't have time on their side. They had to chart out their next move carefully.

'What if she's already sold the details of the antidote?'

'There's only one way to find out,' Aryaman shrugged.

11

Mumbai

Aryaman had requested his mother that they return to Jyoti's apartment. The cops were done sweeping it for evidence, and there was no reason to stay away from it anymore. When Aryaman entered the place, he was overcome by a wave of nostalgia. The apartment felt lived-in, in a good way. He could still sense Jyoti's presence here. He imagined her pacing around the apartment with excitement, as she would whenever she came upon a story that no other journalist but she could have scored. His eyes fell on a portrait of his son as a baby. He picked it up and placed it back, snapping himself out of his thoughts. He had some serious work to do.

Randheer was in the kitchen, helping Aarti with the dinner. Aryaman went into Aditya's room.

Using his gaming console, Aditya had logged in to a secret chat room. Aryaman was stunned at the ease with which Aditya broke through the virtual world's defences and entered the Dark Web. Punching in the code that was scribbled on the documents they got from Ehsaan, he sent a request to chat with Avantika. They waited together for a few minutes but received no response.

'Let's wait it out,' Aryaman said. 'There's no option.'

At the dinner table, Aryaman was quiet, while Randheer made small talk with Aarti. Aditya, seeing his father silent, tried to draw him into conversation.

'Dad, how much do you know about the Dark Web?'

Without forethought, Aryaman snapped at him, 'As much as you do about prisons.'

He immediately realized his response was out of line. This was his son's first genuine attempt at breaking the ice, and he had fended it off without even thinking. He swallowed the mouthful of home-cooked dal chawal, his first good meal in ages, and apologized immediately to his son. Then he abruptly stood up and, to the surprise of the rest of the company, took off his shirt. There were scars all over his torso. Despite everything, though, he had managed to stay fit. He turned to reveal the tattoo on his right shoulder blade. It was a fairly simple outline of a phoenix with the

Roman numeral 'I' in the centre. Randheer looked at it and immediately understood what it meant.

'You see that tattoo, son? You want one like it?'

'What is it?' Aditya asked, intrigued.

'It's a phoenix,' Aryaman said. 'Long ago, when I was in London with Randheer Uncle and a few of our friends, we got piss drunk and played a game of Truth or Dare.'

'Oh, you grown-ups play that too?'

'Yes.' Aryaman grinned. 'Well, I was dared to get a tattoo. It was a relatively free day. So, Randheer here accompanied me to a cheap tattoo parlour and insisted that I get one made. I tried to resist.'

Aditya traced his finger over the tattoo. 'It's pretty cool. Can I get one like it too?'

'No way.' Aryaman laughed. 'No tattoos, no Truth or Dare, no getting drunk for you.'

Aditya pursed his lips, matching his father's sarcasm. 'Then no Dark Web for you either.'

'I hope this Avantika responds,' Aryaman said, putting his shirt back on.

Mahim was the perfect place to hide for Avantika. A crowded, cramped and relatively inexpensive part of Mumbai where different communities had settled in their little pockets. The Christians, the Hindus and the Muslims, all had their own ghettos in Mahim.

Avantika had bought herself a burqa and, for a nominal amount, rented a small room in a hotel adjacent to a shrine of a Muslim saint, which received visitors in large numbers every day.

Though she had figured out a way to hide, Avantika still didn't know what her next move should be. She decided the right thing to do was to get the next available flight out of the city. It wouldn't be a permanent solution, of course, but it would buy her time. She had nobody she could trust. Her own colleagues could be part of the conspiracy that had got the two scientists killed. She couldn't take the risk of going to anyone for help. With her mind refusing to function optimally, Avantika approached a travel agent, hoping he could help her forge travel documents too. She was about to step into his office when her phone buzzed. She saw a notification that made her freeze. It was a chat request from Jyoti on the gaming software. Avantika was aware of Jyoti's death. *This is it,* she thought. *They've found me, and they are going to kill me . . .*

Suffocated, she lifted her veil to take a deep breath and calm herself down. After some thought, she decided to get back to the seedy hotel she was staying at. She clutched her phone tightly as she read and reread the notification several times over. Finally, she decided to play ball.

Who is this?

She didn't have to wait long for the reply.

I am Jyoti's husband. Please get on the system and call me.

She certainly hadn't expected this. But it seemed to be the only way to move forward. Otherwise she would be stuck in a limbo, not knowing whether she was in danger or out of it. At least she had to try to determine the identity of the person trying to contact her.

Okay. Are you using a VPN?

She set up her iPad and logged in to the system. Within minutes, she activated the chat room and saw that Jyoti's username was online. She accepted the request for a video call and put her veil back on.

The grainy live-video feed showed a tired, weak-looking man. She noticed his gaunt face and the slouch in his posture.

'I am Aryaman,' he said flatly. 'Jyoti's no more, as you may be aware. My son told me how to break in through this system and chat with you.'

Avantika was silent.

'I know it's a little difficult for you to trust me,' he continued. 'But I have lost my wife. And I know your story. The dead scientists. Operation Vishaanu. All of it.'

The name Vishaanu sent a shudder down Avantika's spine.

'Please tell me where you are,' Aryaman said. 'Maybe we can meet and talk.'

'Wouldn't that be simple?' She'd spoken for the first time. 'Lead me into a trap and eliminate me too?'

'It would,' Aryaman said. 'But that's not why I am calling you. I am looking for the people who killed my wife. And I will do anything to "eliminate" them, as you put it.'

He could imagine her scornful expression behind the veil.

'Who do you think you are?' she scoffed.

'I was a secret agent for our country. These men don't know who they have set off after them. I just need you to point me in the right direction with whatever you know. And I will save you from any harm coming your way.'

Aryaman's voice sounded shaky but resolute.

'Are you sure we aren't being tapped?'

'You've set this profile up on an email address that you have never shared with anyone, right?'

Avantika nodded.

'And you've not used your cellphone network since?'

'Since Sunil's death,' she responded.

'And you're using a VPN now?'

'Hell, I asked you if you took these precautions!'

'Of course,' he said. 'Then we're not being tapped. Tell me where you are and I will come and get you to safety. My bosses at IRW will take you in and figure the right way out. No foul play, I assure you.'

Her scepticism dropped a notch. This was still an uncertain situation for her, but Aryaman's earnestness was something she could sense, even through this patchy video link.

'Let's face it, Avantika, I am your only option.'

'Okay,' she said. 'Sending you an address. And instructions on how to find me.'

It was a sweltering afternoon. Aryaman stepped out of the car and walked through a packed lane. His eyes scanned for a certain Jaffer Miyan Restaurant as he took a drag of his cigarette. Shopkeepers called out to him in their bids to sell the nauseatingly sweet ittar perfumes and baskets full of roses to place over the saint's tomb inside the dargah. He ignored them as his gaze finally settled on a decrepit food joint, which seemed to have been infested with flies. Homeless men crouched outside in rows, waiting to be fed. He drew closer and was welcomed, rather boisterously, by a man dressed in a vest and torn pyjama.

'Salaam brother,' the waiter said. 'How many fakirs will you feed?'

'Twenty,' Aryaman said.

A burqa-clad woman entered the joint, as if on cue. 'Make that twenty-five, brother. My husband is stingy sometimes. Even with his charity.'

The waiter grinned. 'Thank you, brother. Twenty-five poor men are going to get a good meal.'

Aryaman paid the waiter and then looked at the woman, bemused. They turned and walked out of the joint as the waiter began to line up twenty-five beggars, who muttered words of gratitude for the gracious couple.

'What was that all about?' Aryaman said. 'You could've recognized me anyway.'

'Yes,' Avantika replied. 'But I didn't have the money to buy myself a meal, because I didn't want to risk being tracked by withdrawing any. And whatever I did have, I was going to use on making my way out of Mumbai.'

She held Aryaman by the arm and led him to the hotel.

'So I went to that restaurant and sat beside those hungry men,' she continued. 'I was late to join the line, but despite that, I got the first meal that someone had donated. Those men just gave it to me. This was just my way of returning the favour.'

'And any reason for asking me to buy twenty-five instead of twenty meals?'

She unlocked the door to her room and entered. Then, she raised the veil of her burqa to reveal her delicate, tired, smiling face. 'That was just for fun.'

Aryaman raised an eyebrow to indicate confusion.

'Never mind,' she said. 'Are you sure you haven't been followed?'

'Not to my knowledge,' Aryaman said, looking out of the window. He took out a cigarette but stopped short of lighting it. Holding up the lighter, he turned to her, as if to ask, 'May I?'

She nodded.

'So, this antidote? The guys who killed the scientists and my wife, they don't have the details on how to produce it?'

'Not yet,' Avantika said. 'Only I do. It's with me on my laptop. Whoever wants this virus will also want the antidote. It's six years of work. But . . .' She went quiet.

'But?' Aryaman asked.

She spoke with uncertainty.

'Even I don't know if it's effective. We tested the virus on lab animals. It worked. The antidote hasn't. I need to modify a strain of . . . Anyway. What comes next?'

Aryaman blew a cloud of smoke. He brushed the moth-eaten curtains aside and saw the dargah, standing tall and radiant in all its glory.

'We need to know who is after this. And for that we need to fish them out. I have an idea.'

'I just want to be safe,' she responded.

Aryaman continued emotionlessly. 'You will. I just need you to be . . . the bait.'

Avantika stood up. It was more of a reflex than a gesture of protest. He motioned her to sit down.

'What do you mean by that?' she asked, still standing.

'Well,' Aryaman said. 'You don't know the people who are after you, right?'

She shook her head and slumped back into the weathered sofa.

'Exactly,' he said. 'But they know who you are and are tracking you. All you need to do is switch on the other phone that you have in your purse.'

'How do you know I have another phone in the purse?'

'I didn't.' He shrugged. 'But you've just confirmed that. Anyway, you wouldn't read my messages on the gaming chat system with your usual phone. I knew you'd have another one.'

Avantika ran her hands through her hair. She was sweating profusely. Aryaman sat next to her and looked right into her hazel eyes.

'Switch on your phone. Let them track you,' he said. 'If they reach out, answer.'

She shook her head determinedly. 'No fucking chance. You're out of your mind!'

'You will tell them that you are willing to sell the antidote,' Aryaman continued. 'Tell them it is theirs for a price. Don't seem like an obstacle that they need to eliminate.'

'I'm not doing this.'

'It's the only way I . . .'

'No!' she cut him off. 'You want me to play into their hands?'

'I will be there at the meeting,' Aryaman said, taking her hands into his. 'I will intercept them with my men. It's the only way I can find the men who killed my wife.'

There were tears in his eyes. She extracted her hands from his firm grip and said, 'Take my phone. Trace them or something.'

'But I will never get to actually find the men responsible. In flesh and blood. They'll vanish the minute they doubt me. This is the only concrete lead we have. We have something they absolutely need. And if we don't use it to fish them out, we might pay a heavy price.'

Avantika picked up her bag, adjusted her burqa, and covered her face again, preparing to leave the room. *I am not taking any chances,* she thought. *This is a sure-shot way to die. And a great way for him to get the antidote's formula from me.*

'You have lost two of your friends. I have lost my wife,' Aryaman continued to beg her. 'Do you think I will let any harm come to you?'

'I don't know you well enough to believe you,' she shot back. 'You have your priorities, I have mine. You want revenge. I want to survive. And I was better off fending for myself. I don't want to be used as "bait". No, thank you very much.'

Aryaman stood between her and the door. His face had reddened and she saw in him a feral madness. He was shaking as he spoke. 'This is not just about you, me and Jyoti. If that virus is used against the citizens of our country, will you be able to live with yourself knowing fully well you could have stopped it?'

Avantika's eyes welled up. She looked as helpless as he did.

'Truth be told,' she said finally, 'I can't help you even if I wanted to.'

Aryaman looked puzzled.

'What do you mean?'

'Do we really need the antidote to do this thing?'

'We will at some point,' he said. 'Not just to pull this thing off convincingly but also as a precaution. If those bastards detonate the bomb with the virus, we need to be prepared with adequate doses of the antidote to neutralize the bioweapon.'

She breathed out sharply.

'There's a special formula that we created for the antidote,' she said. 'It's rather complex. There are three vials that have already been produced. And the formula, which is recorded in a file of documents, is locked away with the vials.'

'Locked away?' Aryaman said. 'That's fine, I guess. We'll go and pick it up.'

She let out a sour laugh. 'It's not that easy. The formula and the vials are stored in an underground chamber.'

'Where?'

'It's a Black Site that the intelligence wing set up for us scientist to operate out of. Appears like a defunct factory from outside. But inside, there are guards manning it. Impenetrable. There's no way you can get in and survive.'

Aryaman absorbed the information and thought if this was a serious setback.

12

Mumbai

The next evening, Aryaman went over the plans of
the Black Site for the umpteenth time. The fate of
his mission depended on him retrieving the antidote
from the underground chamber. From what he had
gathered after reconnaissance with Randheer, getting
into the Black Site was not as tough as getting
out of it. He realized that there were probably four officers
who guarded the perimeter of the mid-sized factory.
There could be more or less, but he couldn't say for
sure based on just one night of surveillance. But he'd
take things at face value for now and prepare mentally
to take on more guards if needed. Avantika had told
him that there were about ten security personnel
stationed between the underground chamber and the
main entrance.

While scanning the area, Randheer had made a breakthrough that would make their job marginally easier. There was a large pipeline that supplied water to the underground chamber, possibly for scientific purposes rather than for drinking. If they disabled the water supply, he could crawl in through the pipeline. Along with Avantika.

At this, there were cries of protest on her part. But she was integral to the plan. In fact, without her being physically present, this entire mission would amount to nothing. The chamber could only unlock either with a key card (which they didn't have and couldn't procure), or with a scan of Avantika's iris.

The trickiest part of executing this dicey plan was creating an adequate diversion to draw the attention of as many guards as possible out towards the road, instead of having them patrol the interiors of the factory. And towards this, Randheer had come up with a wild solution. When he presented it to Aryaman, he was met with a glare that seemed to suggest anger as well as ridicule.

A short argument later, Randheer spat out, 'Well, if you have a better plan, I am all ears.'

Having tried and failed to come up with something better, Aryaman finally conceded that Randheer's idea was truly ingenious, though he still worried about its possible consequences.

'Don't worry.' Randheer placed a hand on Aryaman's shoulder. 'This is the best way to divert the guards' attention. You go in through the pipe with Avantika. I'll manage the rest with . . .'

'Nothing should happen to them, Randheer,' Aryaman said through gritted teeth. 'Or else I will bring hell down upon you.'

It was a few minutes past six in the evening when Aarti and Aditya jostled their way through a packed crowd and boarded the local air-conditioned bus headed towards Navi Mumbai on the outskirts of the city. Aarti and Aditya grabbed the first seat they spotted as the electronic door closed behind them.

Aditya had his earphones on and his head resting against the window. Aarti leaned back in her seat, her eyes closed.

A while later, the constant chatter in the bus came to a sudden halt. The passengers had seen what had just happened. A man in a hoodie had stood up and taken the bus conductor hostage, holding a gun to his head. The hijacker had his face covered with a mask, with only a slit for him to see through. He also had a pair of sunglasses on, in order to prevent anyone from getting a good look at his eyes.

The passengers began to shriek. Aarti was silent but shocked. She clutched Aditya's arm. The man pointed the gun at her and gestured for her to stand up.

Trembling, she did as she was instructed. He grabbed her, held a gun to her head and walked towards the bus driver's seat. The driver, a portly old man, looked frightened.

'Don't worry,' the hijacker growled. 'Just drive the bus. I'll tell you where to go. And nobody gets hurt. Don't stop the vehicle and lock all the doors.'

The driver did as he was told.

When the gunman returned to the back of the bus, there was a strained silence.

'I have a very simple demand,' he said. 'It's a plain and simple robbery. Nobody gets hurt if you all cooperate.' He then opened a bag and held it out.

As he looked at the hijacker, Aditya tried hard not to seem too amused. He thought Randheer had put on a rather unconvincing act, but it was working nonetheless.

The masked Randheer looked out of the windshield and saw that the bus was fast approaching the factory. He turned to the hostages and pointed at his open rucksack.

'Money, valuables, mobile phones,' he said aggressively. 'Do what I tell you and you will all be free soon. Come on, this won't take more than half an hour.'

'This can't take more than half an hour,' Aryaman said as he tugged the rusty lid off the pipeline. A flood of water came gushing out. 'It won't take them long to realize that the water supply has been disabled. We have to act within that window.'

He crawled into the pipeline, with Avantika in tow. Aryaman was brisk, so Avantika had some catching up to do as they waded through the wet darkness. Within five minutes, they had made their way to the end of the pipeline. Aryaman, with all his strength, turned a valve around and pushed open the lid. He climbed out of the pipeline and found himself in what looked like a storeroom. When he helped Avantika out, she was drenched and panting.

'It's okay,' he said reassuringly. 'Keep your gun ready. You see anyone, just shoot.'

'I don't think I can . . .'

'It's only going to put them to sleep,' Aryaman said. 'You're not killing anyone.'

'I've never done this before,' she said.

'I usually shoot to kill, so I can't say the same.' Aryaman cocked his tranquillizer gun and kept it at the ready. 'Come on, follow my lead.'

Aryaman tiptoed towards the door and opened it an inch. Outside, the staircase to the basement with the secure chamber was being manned by two guards. Aryaman pressed his ear against the door to hear them speak on their walkie-talkies. Through the crackle of their handsets, he heard something about a civilian bus having been hijacked nearby. The guards, however, were told not to move from their positions.

The ones outside the factory were looking into the situation.

Aryaman shook his head in disbelief. 'I can't believe I've just allowed my mother and son to be taken hostage . . .'

'And they are being used as human shields,' Avantika said sarcastically, 'by your friend. So that should make you feel better.'

Aryaman shook his head. 'It doesn't. Anyway, time to get to business.'

He pulled out a pistol from a holster at his ankle. This one had real bullets. *If shit did go down,* he thought, *I'd prefer putting these guys to sleep for good.*

'On my count.' He stared at Avantika. 'Three . . . Two . . . One!'

He kicked the door open and, with two clean shots, fired at the two guards with his tranquillizer gun. Both were shot in the face. Dazed, the guards tried to reach for their weapons. But Aryaman charged head first at them and rammed one guard into the wall. Avantika took several shots at the other guard, until he collapsed.

Avantika's hands were trembling.

'Well, he's going to sleep like a baby,' Aryaman said.

He searched both the bodies and found no key card. He picked up their walkie-talkies, destroying one and keeping the other to listen in on the instructions the remaining guards were receiving. He then went for their guns, dismantling them and holding on to the cartridges. If the two guards were to regain consciousness, which was unlikely, he didn't want them firing at him.

'Lead.' Aryaman pointed at the staircase. 'I'll cover you, don't worry about it.'

Avantika went forward, her legs shaking.

They went down a short flight of stairs. When they reached the landing, Aryaman told Avantika to wait and stuck his neck out to survey the area. It was a large room, sanitized and brightly lit like a hospital facility. There were a few tables with lab equipment placed on them. A narrow passage at the opposite end of the room led to the chamber that held the antidote. Three guards—tough-looking guys—were in position here. They sat on their chairs, talking to each other.

'Okay, this is it,' Aryaman whispered to Avantika. 'The minute I move towards them, you rush to the corner of the room and take cover behind that table.'

'Do I tell Randheer we are in?'

Aryaman nodded. 'As soon as I knock them out, you rush towards me and unlock that door. We take that antidote and then run through the exit at the back.'

He held his gun firmly and crept into the room, taking cover behind the furniture. Avantika followed his lead. 'You sure you can handle three of them?'

'Shouldn't you have asked me this before we entered?' he asked with a wry smile. 'But let's find out.'

The next moment, he picked up a Bunsen burner and flung it to his right. Two guards stood up immediately and rushed towards the source of the noise while

Aryaman took cover behind some furniture. The third guard ran the other way, towards the reinforced-steel door shielding the antidote. Aryaman raised his gun and took a shot at a guard's shin; the man instantly fell to the ground. The other guard fired several rounds at Aryaman, who somersaulted out of range, evading the onslaught of bullets that smashed the lab equipment to smithereens. With one well-aimed shot to the shoulder, Aryaman took this guard out as well.

The third guard was hurriedly inserting a card into the slot that controlled the door. Aryaman realized he was trying to disable the system and to lock the door in a way that even Avantika's iris wouldn't be able to open it. He turned to Avantika and said, 'Go shoot these two and neutralize them now!'

Avantika picked up her tranquillizer gun and scampered towards the two injured guards. Hesitantly, she shot one of them in the chest. She then aimed at the other guy, who was trying to get to his feet, pressing the wound on his bleeding shoulder. But she was out of darts. The guard grunted and charged at her. She leapt back towards the table, picked up some test tubes and flung them at him. That didn't seem to have any effect. He grabbed her by her hair and slammed her against the wall. She got winded. The guard picked up his gun and aimed at her head. A shot rang out, but it wasn't him who had pulled the trigger! Avantika had fired at his kneecap, with a gun she had concealed in her jacket. She hadn't wanted it on her, but Aryaman had insisted upon it. The guard yelled in pain and fell backwards.

Aryaman, too, was in the middle of a scuffle. The brawny guard had hit several punches that had thrown Aryaman off balance. But he fought back and landed a set of hard jabs himself. Avantika's gunshot had distracted Aryaman. And this gave the guard an opportunity to launch a devastating kick into his ribs. Aryaman slumped to the ground, coughing and spitting blood as he watched the guard pull out his keycard. He was about to swipe it when Aryaman sprang to his feet and, with great force, delivered a hard blow to the back of the guard's skull. The card was still in the slot, almost midway through the swipe. Aryaman took the card out and kept kicking the man until he lost consciousness. He then called out to Avantika, who scurried towards him.

'Quick,' he said. 'Unlock the door.'

Avantika rushed towards it and punched in a code. A software to scan her iris came up on the display.

'I hope they haven't deleted my details from the database.'

Aryaman looked at her, aghast. 'And you mention this now? Could they have?'

'Yes,' she said worriedly. 'I'm sorry! I'm new to this!'

She walked up to the scanner. Aryaman looked on tensely for the next few seconds. He hadn't thought of that possibility. Clearly, nobody else had either. The door slid open after the software recognized Avantika's iris. She smiled for the first time since he had seen her. A cloud of steam burst out, and when it cleared away, it revealed the antidote: a set of vials delicately placed on a stand.

Avantika called Randheer.

'We're in,' she said. 'Should be out in the next five minutes. How are you holding up?'

She heard Randheer laughing. 'Aryaman's kid is one hell of an actor. He is out of the bus and has managed to draw all the guards towards us, as planned.'

Aryaman lifted the antidote and the file that held the formula. A second later, a blaring alarm went off. The door began to slide shut. He grabbed Avantika by her wrist and rushed towards the opening. But Avantika tripped and fell. The door had all but crushed her foot when Aryaman blocked it with the unconscious guard's gun until she dragged herself out.

'Fuck,' he muttered. 'There will be backup in no time. And they are going to be here to kill us, not capture. Just follow me!'

He rushed back up the staircase as Avantika struggled to keep up. Aryaman saw a door burst open and several guards run in. He fired at them, not allowing them to assess the situation. Running towards the back door, he fired at them continuously. Finally, he pushed Avantika out and made his own exit.

A sedan sped towards them and came to a halt near the door. Randheer was in the car, with Aditya.

Aryaman fired at the guards as Avantika got in. Then he, too, leapt in. The car sped past the bus that had all the hostages. The guards continued to fire away at them. Aryaman carefully held the vials and placed them in Randheer's bag, which also carried the loot from his bus heist.

'Where's Mom?' Aryaman asked, his mouth agape.

'One of the guards held her back,' Randheer said, slamming the steering wheel. 'To question her.'

Aryaman punched the seat in frustration. 'Fuck!'

13

Istanbul, Turkey

Eymen and Asra drove towards the port of Istanbul. A large part of their mission depended on this phase going right. Asra kept her eyes peeled throughout their journey for any car that could be tailing them. They were supposed to meet Lior at the port. He had, for an astronomical amount, helped put together a plan to get the weapon out of Turkey. The money did not worry Asra, since her bosses trusted Lior to do his job well. What mattered most to her was getting the weapon smuggled out. And she couldn't rely on bullish Eymen when it came to making tactical decisions.

At one point, Eymen wanted to smuggle the weapon by air. He had expressly stated that he didn't trust this Lior fellow. 'A person who does things for money alone can never be trusted. What if he took an amount from the enemy to sell us out too? If he isn't driven by his ideologies, he isn't to be relied upon,' Eymen had argued.

He could be right, Asra had thought at the time. But Lior was their best bet. And that is what everything in intelligence comes down to: the best bet. Not necessarily the safest one.

Asra lit a cigarette and strolled casually towards the rendezvous point once Eymen had parked the vehicle. She saw the beautiful expanse of the sea before her and took in the view. The birds chirping, the balmy wind. This, she thought, was the serenity that the earth offered to those who sought it.

Eymen nudged her, and Asra broke out of her daze, reminding herself that she was here for another purpose. She looked at him, letting out a puff of smoke. He pointed at a drab cargo ship. Lior, flanked by two of his huge bodyguards, was waving at them from its deck.

Lior didn't really need bodyguards, but he kept them for the same reason some people bought ornaments. He could well take down two people at the same time by himself. But why bother when you can pay someone to do that for you? Lior was a dangerous man who dealt in the machinery of war all around the world. But he was also faceless in many senses. People had heard of him, but no one ever quite got a good look at him. Intelligence agencies had an old file photo of him. But he no longer resembled the man they had photographed. Money can buy a lot of things: fake hair, higher cheekbones, a cleft in one's chin, you name it. For his part, Lior had no other reason than money to be in this particular deal. So far, he had got what was promised. And so he delivered.

Had Eymen and Asra not kept their end of the deal, he would have had to resort to some unsavoury means. He had enough resources to do that. If he needed to pick a beef with someone in the PIA, he always had someone else in a rival agency to help him get what he needed.

Eymen and Asra walked up the rickety ramp that led to the cargo ship. Lior greeted them with a wide smile and a friendly handshake. He sensed that they weren't in the mood for conversation. Nor was he, to be honest. So they spoke very little as they made their way to a large, damp, secluded room stacked with crates.

'Welcome to the presidential suite,' he said mockingly. His joke didn't have an audience in Eymen and Asra, of course. Their eyes scanned the musty room, looking past the mice scuttling by, for the crate that mattered.

'It's right here,' Lior said, leading them to it. It was an ordinary-looking crate. He lifted the lid off it. There were rows of perfume bottles, neatly arranged. Lior moved those aside to reveal a metal container with a keypad panel meant to punch in a passcode. He entered the combination slowly, so that Eymen and Asra could make note, and opened the door to reveal the vials of death.

'The best Turkish delight money can buy you,' he sniggered. 'Here, put in a passcode of your own and we're good.'

Lior made an exaggerated show of turning around as Asra did the needful.

'Anything from the girl? Advani?' she asked.

Lior paused. Eymen watched him with suspicion as Lior turned theatrically around.

'I was hoping you'd ask . . .'

'Did you hear from her?' Eymen stepped towards him, his voice gruff.

'Calm down, big boy. Always ready to bite someone's head off!'

He enjoyed riling Eymen up. Asra was replacing the perfumes into the crate, with her back turned towards them. Lior pointed at her derrière and winked at Eymen.

'Maybe you should blow off some steam,' Lior mocked him. 'Can really help calm one down. Trust me!'

Asra turned around to see a red-faced Eymen clenching his fists.

'Lior,' she said. 'Quit fucking around. Tell me about it.'

Lior's posture straightened. He meant business.

'Funnily enough,' he said. 'I didn't have to look too hard for her. She reached out to me earlier today.'

Asra took an agitated step towards him.

'And you didn't tell us about this until we asked?'

Lior pursed his lips and shrugged.

'Calm down,' he said. 'It's good news. She sounded scared. And here's the fun bit . . .'

'Get on with it before I bash your fucking brains out,' Eymen growled.

'She wants to cut a deal,' he said. 'Money in exchange for the details of the antidote. I have to get back to her with the price I can pay. I suspect she will negotiate. She sounded frightened.'

'She's ballsy.' Asra smiled. 'She knows whoever has taken the virus will also want to know how to control it. And she'd rather not die like her colleagues. Instead, she wants to make money off it.'

Eymen lit himself a cigarette. This was good news.

'Once she names her price,' Asra said, 'I will wire the money to you. The sooner she gets back, the better.'

Lior gave a nod and shook hands with Asra. He didn't look at Eymen as he began to leave. Then he turned around and smiled.

'Bon voyage,' he said. 'Get in touch with me once you reach your destination. I will have an update on Dr Advani by then.'

Mumbai

'Your plan was garbage,' Aryaman said, kicking a chair in frustration. 'How the fuck do we get Mom out?'

Randheer bit his lip. Avantika watched on, another silent spectator. Aditya, who had been sitting morosely through most of the conversation, smirked upon hearing the expletive.

'Not in front of the kid.' Randheer clucked his tongue and walked towards Aryaman to calm him down. But Aryaman pushed him away.

'It's okay,' Randheer continued. 'I've spoken to my bosses. The cops will release her in no time. They are holding her to get a better description of the mad dude on the bus. She's not being treated badly.'

'My problem isn't how she is being treated, Randheer. My mom is tough as nails. The problem is that they will know she is my mom. And then they will be on to me and realize that I have stolen the antidote. The news will travel far and wide, and I'll be shipped back to a jail. That is my fucking problem.'

Aditya shook his head disapprovingly. 'Language, Dad.'

Aryaman breathed out sharply and, despite himself, smiled at his son. He lit a cigarette and said to Randheer with an air of finality, 'Better get my mom out of there before the agency learns of my involvement.'

His attention shifted to Avantika. She looked pale and exhausted, her hair dishevelled and eyes bloodshot. He couldn't begin to imagine what she was going through. But he didn't want to imagine it either. Now was not the time for sentiment.

'Did Lior get back?' his tone was softer towards her.

She shrugged and began to look around for her phone.

'Great, you haven't even been checking your damn phone,' Aryaman said, losing his patience. 'He is our only lead to the bioweapon. And you aren't even keeping an eye out.'

Aditya got up and held his father's hands firmly.

'Dad,' he said. 'Calm down.'

Aryaman regarded his son and felt a moment of relief. He hadn't known before this that the words spoken by his child could have a soothing effect on him. He was finally building a relationship with his son, he thought. Not under ideal circumstances, but life was often far from ideal.

Avantika threw Aryaman an aggrieved look as she picked up her phone. Nothing from Lior.

'I have lost my wife,' Aryaman said. 'I lost my friends. My mentor. I don't know what is going to happen to my mother. It's a little tough to calm down, son.'

Avantika's phone buzzed. She picked it up immediately. When she read the message, her eyes widened. It was from Lior, but what he wanted from her was something they hadn't prepared for.

'What is it?' Randheer asked. 'Read it out loud.'

Avantika gulped and read out the message in her shaky voice.

I want you to meet me in Istanbul at the earliest with the documents. No funny business. You and I meet face to face. I get the formula for the antidote and you get the money.

'He wants her to go to Istanbul!' Randheer was shocked. 'I thought he'd set up a rendezvous point in India itself. This is dangerous, Aryaman. Our mission isn't sanctioned for us to make such decisions . . .'

Aryaman raised a hand in the air to stop him from speaking. Everyone was silent and all eyes were on Aryaman. He looked out of the window for an entire minute and then, with his back turned towards them, said one word.

'Deal.'

'Excuse me?'

'Avantika.' He glared at her. 'We are going to Istanbul.'

14

Istanbul, Turkey

Aryaman had spent most of the flight telling Avantika what her demeanour should be like and where he would be when she is passing over the details of the antidote to Lior. He made her repeat the plan several times over and only then allowed her to sleep.

From his window seat, Aryaman looked listlessly at the plane's wing, fighting the urge to smoke. Arranging the trip hadn't been as troublesome as he had expected. Randheer had managed to pull a few strings and to procure for Aryaman and Avantika fake identities—courtesy of the agency—along with the plane tickets. What did worry Randheer, however, was the fact that he needed to get Aryaman's mother and son back to Dehradun in one piece and have them stay there until all of this was over.

Randheer was hopeful that this would end pretty soon. If he managed to figure out who had bought the bioweapon from Lior, he could pass on the information to the people he believed would take the right action. He and Aryaman would then step back. Considering the severity of the situation, he was hopeful that insubordination would be punished with just a rap on the knuckles for both of them. He hadn't told Aryaman, of course. Aryaman was against approaching the agency for any help, holding a grudge and rightly so. Aryaman's words, uttered before he stepped in to catch his flight, still resonated in Randheer's ears.

'If shit hits the fan,' he had said in his gravelly voice. 'Take care of Mom and Aditya. If you feel you owe me anything, this is it.'

The odds were stacked against Aryaman in Turkey. He could see Avantika's entire frame trembling as she made her way towards the rooftop cafeteria where she was meeting Lior. Aryaman assured her that he had her back. But in a situation like this, words weren't really going to comfort her. Not when she was striking a bogus deal with an international arms dealer.

The Hagia Sophia monument in Istanbul appeared unforgettably stunning in the warm, orange glow of the evening. But Avantika, unlike the other tourists, wasn't marvelling at its beauty or its imposing structure. She chose a table in the corner of the rooftop cafeteria. As soon as she took her seat, almost as if on cue, Lior stepped out of the designated smoking area and greeted her with a smile that scared her.

'I've been waiting for you,' he said as he walked towards her, flanked by his emotionless beefcakes. 'You're two minutes before time. Impressive.'

Avantika shrugged. 'I wouldn't turn up late for a deal that is about to get me this much money.'

Lior smiled, turned to one of his men and whispered something that Avantika couldn't quite make out. It made her nervous. He had a repulsive quality about him, although there was nothing physically off-putting in his appearance. He dragged a chair and eased himself into it, sitting right across from her. He took off his shades with a flourish and examined her. Following his gaze as it ran down to her neckline, she felt her body stiffen. She looked at her watch and then back at him immediately. Pale, but trying hard to maintain her composure, she smiled at him. Then, to Avantika's relief, a waiter strode over to their table with two cups of coffee. Lior pushed one cup towards her.

'I took the liberty of ordering you a special local coffee.' He grinned. 'All that travelling must have been tiring.'

Avantika didn't even look at the cup. 'I'm good. Let's talk shop.'

Lior laughed exaggeratedly and shook his head in a show of regret.

'And then women say men have lost their manners.' Lior clucked his tongue. 'No place for old-world charm anymore, is there?'

Avantika looked at her watch again.

'Are you getting late?' Lior's smile had vanished.

Avantika countered the question with another question, 'The money?'

Lior snapped his fingers at his guard, who placed a briefcase on the table. Avantika snapped it open. The money was there, as promised.

'Now it's your turn,' Lior said and drained all his coffee in one gulp.

Avantika, without a moment of hesitation, picked up her handbag, unzipped it and pulled out an iPad. She unlocked the device and held it out to him.

'What if the device tracks my movements once I am out of here?' he asked hesitantly, raising an eyebrow at her.

Avantika looked at him, dead in the eye.

'That would be as bad as signing my own death warrant, wouldn't it?'

There was something about Avantika, about her confidence, that didn't feel right to Lior. And then he looked at her eyes shift towards her watch yet again. Nevertheless, he took the iPad from her and opened the file she had pointed to. He studied it for a few minutes and then casually said to her, 'Seems genuine. But we aren't done yet.'

The colour drained from her face. 'What do you mean?'

He flashed his dirty grin. 'I am going to need you to come with me to my facility. You prepare a batch of the antidote for me. I will test it and if it works, you are off the hook and free to enjoy the money.'

Avantika froze. She was not prepared for this. And as a matter of fact, nor was Aryaman, who dropped all pretence of blending in as a tourist the minute he heard Lior reveal his plan. He began to rush towards the rooftop cafeteria, pressing on the earpiece to hear the conversation playing out.

'You're wearing a nice watch,' Lior's voice crackled through Aryaman's earpiece. 'Your friends, if they can hear this through that tiny bug in your watch, should know that they can't outwit me. Let them pick you up once you have made me an antidote that works!'

Aryaman looked up at Lior, who, having thrown Avantika's watch down, stood on the balcony, staring right back at him. Lior's guards were manhandling Avantika. Aryaman ran towards them, but Lior pulled out a gun and fired three shots in the air, with no real intention of harming anyone. Just causing chaos until he slipped away. People began to rush frenziedly around, screaming for help. Aryaman, caught in the crowd like a fish swimming upstream, kept an eye on

Avantika and saw her being shoved into an SUV. Lior took his seat at the wheel and the car set off.

Aryaman saw a policeman climb off his bike and rush to control the crowd. Going with his instinct and choosing what seemed like his only option, he knocked the cop right to the ground unconscious. He took the cop's pistol and key and hopped on to the bike. Three other policemen, who had witnessed all this, came to the conclusion that Aryaman was the cause for the chaos. As Aryaman started the bike and began to chase down Lior's vehicle, the cops called for backup to go after him.

The streets of Istanbul had seen nothing like this before. Aryaman's Turkish police-issued bike swerved past traffic in pursuit of Lior's bulky BMW SUV. Lior drove rashly past the other cars, even bumping them out of the way when required. Aryaman controlled the bike with one hand as he aimed and fired at the SUV, shattering its rear window. He didn't want to shoot again lest he injure Avantika.

Lior ducked for cover in his car, dragging Avantika down with him. His men pulled out their weapons and fired at Aryaman. But Aryaman was quick to move to the other side of the road. But now he faced the oncoming traffic. Though he had made it tougher for Lior's men to fire at him, he now had to manoeuvre his way through vehicles speeding towards him. At the same time, a BMW SUV identical to Lior's car had joined the other lane. Two men rolled down the windows of this SUV and opened fire indiscriminately in Aryaman's direction, not quite caring if they hit others. All around them, vehicles screeched to a halt and pedestrians ran for cover.

Aryaman took careful aim and shot the driver of the other SUV square in the head. The car swerved and rammed into the side of a building. Aryaman saw his chance to pursue Lior's vehicle, which had sped away and had just taken a sharp right into a narrow lane. Aryaman could smell the burning rubber and hear the sharp sirens of the police vehicles that had joined the chase. He knew how things stood. He was a man who had assaulted a cop. It wasn't going to go down well. He looked back to see the police firing at his bike's wheels. Drifting into the narrow lane, which was occupied by some ice-cream vendors, he saw the SUV exit the lane at the other end and enter the main road again. Aryaman followed as quickly as he could. He revved the bike and almost caught up with the SUV. He fired three bullets at its wheels. After the third shot, Lior's car spiralled out of control and rammed into an oncoming police car.

Aryaman braked hard and a police car hit his bike from behind, catapulting him into the air. He raised and joined his elbows to protect himself from landing head first. The fall was agonizingly painful, nevertheless. He had landed hard, tearing his shirt and scraping the skin on his forearms. He struggled to his feet and turned to see the Turkish cops aiming their guns at him and at

Lior, who was stepping out of his car, holding a gun to Avantika's head.

Aryaman and Lior glared at each other. The cops formed a circle around them, yelling out warnings for them to not move.

'A step closer and I blow her brains out,' Lior announced. 'Let me leave and nobody dies!'

Aryaman took a step towards him, his pistol at the ready.

'Go on,' he growled. 'Let me see you do it.'

Avantika was petrified. 'Aryaman.' Her lips quivered. 'What . . . What do you mean?'

Aryaman smirked as he took another step towards Lior.

'So that's your name, huh? Aryaman?' Lior smiled.

'Do it. Or I kill her instead. And you don't get the formula to produce the antidote.'

Lior's finger was on the trigger. Avantika wheezed with fear. The cops were screaming at Aryaman to stand down, but he paid no heed to them.

'Or,' Aryaman said as he walked closer to Lior. 'I walk up to you. Get into the car with you. We get away from these men and get her to produce the antidote for us. We sell it and split the money. All three of us win.'

'STAND DOWN OR I SHOOT!' a cop bellowed through the megaphone. 'THIS IS YOUR FINAL WARNING!'

'Sounds like he means business,' Aryaman said to Lior, cool as a cucumber. 'What's it gonna be? We can get back into the car and we can speed out of here together.'

Lior seemed to consider. He nodded at Aryaman and took a step back towards the car. Aryaman smiled. But his mind was doing the math. He knew he had nothing more than a split second to act. And that split second would be make-or-break.

As soon as Lior's body tilted a little to shove Avantika back into the car, Aryaman spotted his chance and took his shot. The bullet grazed past Avantika's leg and lodged itself into Lior's shin. Both of them shrieked in pain, almost in unison. Aryaman, seeing Lior aim back at him, fired again. This time the bullet hit Lior's gun, sending it flying out of his hand and wounding his fingers.

Aryaman saw that the cops were about to open fire when he turned to them and raised his hands to surrender. He dropped his gun and fell to his knees, interlocking his fingers behind his head. The cops rushed to him and kicked him to the ground. He felt his bloody arms being twisted and the cuffs being tightened around his wrists. He turned to look at Avantika, who had fainted and was being taken to a police vehicle.

Lior, despite the pain he felt, looked at Aryaman venomously.

'I will end you,' he spat out.

'Many have tried.'

Lior was handcuffed and made to sit in a little, stuffy room at a small safe house that the Turkish intelligence had whisked them away to. He leaned forward on the table, looking his Turkish interrogator straight in the eye. He wasn't perturbed at all, even though this was the first time he'd found himself in such a messy situation. The authorities went through his papers—which, of course, were fake—but found nothing alarming in them. Despite the pressure they put him under, he wasn't breaking. It was Aryaman who knew about Lior's true identity, beyond the fake name on his passport.

So the one person who could get Lior to break was waiting outside the room, smoking a cigarette. Aryaman smoked despite the man in charge of the unit requesting him not to. Avantika sat beside him, a thick layer of gauze wrapped around her injured leg. She was shaken up, but Aryaman ignored her and focused on the thoughts swirling in his head. He was somewhat stressed out. A call to the Indian embassy had led the Turkish officials to an agent only too keen to help Aryaman and Avantika: Randheer.

Back home, Randheer was in a soup. He had no choice but to tell his higher-ups, who weren't big fans of his anyway, about all that had transpired. Bipin Sharma's immediate remark was that they should never have released Aryaman in the first place. But Randheer, thanks to a few supportive people in the system, managed to get the authorities to transfer Aryaman's mother and son back to Dehradun.

The Turkey fracas was a tougher one to manage, but Randheer did his bit by communicating to the officers in Istanbul a message supposedly from the Indian intelligence. He told them that one of their men, Aryaman, had nabbed an international gun dealer. Now all they needed in return was permission for their agent to interrogate this dealer. After that, the Turks could keep Lior in their custody and even claim internationally that they were the ones who had caught the elusive bastard. After half an hour of deliberation and working all the angles, the Turkish intelligence gave in.

Aryaman entered the interrogation room, holding the door open for the two Turkish officers to step out. He walked up to the wall, dismantled the CCTV camera and turned to Lior.

'Good cop, bad cop.' Lior smiled. 'Cute.'

Aryaman dragged his chair towards Lior, lit himself a cigarette and sat down.

'You won't find anything about this cute once I'm done with you.'

There was a small cloud of smoke between the two.

'I've already said what I had to.' Lior shrugged. 'I'm just a businessman.'

Aryaman took a key out of his pocket and unlocked Lior's handcuffs. He then knelt down and undid the chains that held Lior to the ground.

'You're in the business of selling death.' Aryaman looked Lior in the eye. 'I am in the business of saving lives.'

Aryaman threw aside the key with the chains and cuffs. Lior stood up and spat on the ground.

'So, let's negotiate.' Aryaman got up as well, cigarette dangling from the corner of his mouth.

Lior rolled up his fists and began to throw punches indiscriminately at Aryaman. The blows hurt but not enough to take Aryaman out of the fight. Lior grabbed him by the neck and pinned him against the wall, tightening his grip around Aryaman's throat.

'It's true,' Aryaman said as his face reddened. 'You really do throw punches like a businessman.'

Aryaman summoned more energy and kneed Lior in the balls. Lior's fighting style was haphazard, and Aryaman could kill him in an instant if he had to. But he needed answers, and the Turks needed Lior alive.

Aryaman elbowed Lior in the face, sending him crashing to the floor. Aryaman picked up his burning cigarette and bent over Lior. He then forced Lior's eye open and stubbed the cigarette in it. Lior screamed in pain. Aryaman crushed Lior's fingers under his boot. Realizing this fight wasn't his to win, Lior stopped resisting.

'Good,' Aryaman said. 'Now you tell me what I need to know. And you'll still live. One hand and one eye intact. A businessman needs at least that to count his money.'

Lior was shaking in pain.

'Tell me everything,' Aryaman continued. 'Or this ends here for you, and I go out and find things out anyway.'

Later that night, Aryaman and Avantika made their way to a local bar and had a few drinks. Randheer had arranged for them a clean exit from Turkey. But what they had learnt from Lior shook them to the core. The clock was ticking, and they knew that if they didn't act in time their country would face the most diabolical bioterrorism attack in recent history.

15

Aditya had managed to grasp the entire situation pretty clearly. His grandmother wanted to make sure that the young boy lived with no misconceptions about the world around him. His father, though a well-meaning man, was a mess. His mother was no more. His grandmother, too, would lose the battle to age in the near future. And his newest friend in Dehradun—the adorable little mutt, Chor—didn't have the life expectancy of a human being.

'Enjoy everything while it lasts,' Aarti said, stroking Aditya's head as he fed Chor yet another batch of the boiled chicken. 'I want to be honest with you, Aditya. Your father is on a mission that may not end well.'

Chor was lapping up the food. Aditya's eyes slowly welled up as his grandmother's words sunk in. He nodded and turned his face away, pretending to scan the books in the children's section of the library.

'Can we go for a walk?' he asked her.

Aarti agreed. They stepped out of the library and watched the Aroras relaxing on the front lawn. There were a few teenagers strumming their guitars and singing a soothing song nearby.

'Just taking my grandson out for a walk.' Aarti beamed at the Aroras. 'Let him see the stark contrast between Mumbai and Dehradun.'

Mr Arora grinned. 'Oh, well! I shudder to think that people actually enjoy living there. Is Chor going along?'

'Of course,' Aditya said, holding Chor's leash. 'My little brother.'

They all laughed.

Aarti led him out, and the two of them—with Chor in tandem—walked down the winding roads as the evening set in. They spoke about many things, in a way they hadn't when Jyoti was alive. They discussed the world of intelligence.

'There is no place where espionage is not possible,' Aarti quoted Sun Tzu as they stopped for coffee. She ordered black coffee, as her son would have, and Aditya went for a frappuccino.

'Granny,' Aditya said tiredly. 'Enough of this spy business. Let's talk about something kids my age are expected to talk about?'

His grandmother laughed heartily. 'I'm afraid I don't know what it is kids your age talk about,' she said, sipping her black coffee and taking short but steady steps ahead on the empty street. 'Would you rather I talk to you about how harmful smoking and drinking is?'

'You could,' Aditya said snidely. 'But it didn't seem to work with Dad.'

Aarti was distracted by something. She looked over her shoulder and said, 'I think we should get back home now, Adi.'

'Why?'

'There are a couple of men following us,' Aarti said. 'I don't think it's anything alarming. They could be some people your father has sent to keep a watch on us.'

'Well, then we are safe, aren't we?'

Aarti turned around yet again. The two men turned right, towards a market. Amateurs, she thought. Had they known the art of tailing someone well enough, they would have continued walking down the road confidently and tried to come across as regular people. Instead, they had made things more obvious by disappearing like this.

'One can never know,' she said. 'Let's go back home and call Randheer.'

IRW headquarters, New Delhi

There was no point holding anything back from the officials. Especially now. It had been a day since Aryaman and Avantika returned from Turkey. Aryaman felt a strange sense of resentment as he walked through the familiar corridors of the IRW headquarters. Randheer knew exactly what he was putting him through when he'd asked him to return, face Sharma and the other officials, and come clean about all that had happened since he had stepped out of prison.

Bipin Sharma hadn't guaranteed that any of Aryaman's actions wouldn't warrant another punishment. But Aryaman had an ace up his sleeve. He was going to negotiate with Sharma before they could send him back to that dreaded prison island.

In the lobby, Aryaman met a harrowed-looking Randheer, who reeked of cigarettes and stale perfume.

'Your mother gave me an earful.' He chuckled nervously, trying to lighten the atmosphere. 'I had kept a two-man team for surveillance on her and the boy. She spotted them and shook them off. She has asked for them to be replaced.'

Aryaman paced towards the room where the meeting with Sharma was supposed to happen. His mind wasn't on his family for now. He had larger concerns— like the safety of his country. He paused right outside the door and took a deep breath. Randheer gave him a reassuring look and thought, *Aryaman would hate to admit it, but he is fucking nervous.*

Randheer pushed the door open and entered first. He saw Sharma sitting alone. There was nobody else in the room. Of course, they would be recording the entire conversation. Aryaman walked in and stood before Sharma.

They looked into each other's eyes unwaveringly. Ignoring Sharma's outstretched arm, more of a formal gesture than an olive branch, Aryaman went straight to his chair.

'Good evening,' Aryaman said. The closest he could get to being formal was with these two sharply uttered words.

'Tell me,' Sharma said. 'What do you know?'

'Lior Meirs, international gunrunner, was the guy who told me what I am about to tell you. A bioweapon is on its way to India. He told me it's being shipped in by a couple. Probably funded by the PIA.'

'Anything else?'

'Only that the attack will happen as soon as it is in the country,' Aryaman said. 'They have planned this out meticulously. And they are ready to die for their cause. Beyond this, he told me nothing about the couple or about what they want.'

Sharma was silent for some time. Then he rubbed the bridge of his nose, closed his eyes and spoke.

'The idea was to create a bioweapon that we could have for dire circumstances,' he said. 'And now it's come back to bite us in the ass. I should never have sanctioned Operation Vishaanu.'

Aryaman scoffed and turned away. Sharma noticed a wry smile on his face.

'You find that funny?' he asked Aryaman.

'Of course, I do. A weak leader questions his own decisions. A strong one, like Amarjyot Sir, would have had more conviction and made sure he saw things through to the end, even if it meant righting his own wrongs.'

Sharma didn't take this well. He leaned forward, trembling with rage.

'And you do know how that ended for him, don't you? Suicide. An escape route only a coward would take.'

Aryaman stood up and slammed his fist on the table. But Randheer held him. 'We have a problem to deal with,' Randheer said, pushing Aryaman back into his chair. 'What's done is done. Let's fight over that once we overcome this fucking situation!'

A long pause ensued. Aryaman unscrewed the cap of a water bottle. He downed the water, crushed the empty bottle and flung it aside.

'What do you propose, Aryaman?' Randheer restarted the conversation.

'These people killed my wife,' Aryaman told Sharma. 'They have made it personal. And nothing you do will stop me from ending them. That's a promise I've made to my son.'

Sharma didn't speak, and Randheer realized there was nothing he could do to contain Aryaman.

'You must be thinking you'll pull another fast one on me and send me back to prison,' Aryaman continued, gnashing his teeth in rage. 'But that isn't going to happen. I have something that we absolutely need to win this battle.'

'And what is that?' Sharma asked, a hint of condescension in his tone.

'Dr Advani's cooperation,' Aryaman said. 'As of now, she is the only one who can effectively produce the antidote. Without her, even if the attack happens, you won't be able to stop it from spreading and killing our citizens.'

'You and Dr Advani can both go to jail together for pulling that stunt. Stealing the antidote.'

'Well, you should protect areas of such importance better then,' Aryaman said. 'Especially if an out-of-the-game spy and a frightened scientist can waltz in and out of them like that!'

Sharma stoically suppressed his urge to respond in kind and said, 'So how can we work on this now, Aryaman? Give me a plan that you think will work.'

Aryaman looked at him and said, 'Patronizing, as usual.'

'Not this time.'

'Is this conversation being recorded?'

'Yes.'

'Two things then, before I start.'

'Shoot.'

'One. I want a copy of this conversation as proof. The videotape. Or else you will turn on your word and say this never happened.'

'Can be done.' He looked at Randheer. 'Please give him the tape. All of it, including his misbehaviour.'

He turned back to Aryaman, 'And the second thing?'

'You protect my family through all of this,' Aryaman said. 'I want agents posted around them at all times. And also around Avantika's next of kin. There's a strong chance we've been exposed through a leak to the PIA after the Turkey incident. Deal?'

Sharma responded immediately, 'Yes. It's a deal.'

Aryaman rolled up his sleeves.

'We need another facility up and active,' Aryaman said. 'We get Avantika to produce as many batches of the antidote as possible. The problem is she doesn't know how effective these will be. There's no knowing when it'll start to fight the virus and how long a human will take to recover after being injected with it. The scientists started dying before they could test all of this, as you may be aware.'

Sharma nodded. 'Done, we bring Avantika in then.'

'Good,' Aryaman said. 'Lior admitted that the weapon is being shipped from Turkey. We aren't sure if the cargo comes to us directly or moves to another ship at any other port. Or if it comes by air.'

'I will alert the security officials at each possible . . .'

'No,' Aryaman said. 'We don't know how deep the conspiracy is. If there are any leaks, the PIA can plan this around in a way that would give us no leads. Let them play out their plan until the weapon is in our country. And then we catch them.'

Sharma stared at Aryaman incredulously. 'So we bring a weapon of mass destruction into our country?'

'We allow it, yes,' Aryaman said somewhat nervously.

'That's ridiculous. This sounds like something your defunct Phoenix 5 group would do. Not me.'

'Listen, sir,' Aryaman said. 'This is our only shot at uncovering the conspiracy. We don't even know if this is PIA acting alone or if there are other elements at play. And they might just have joined hands. My point is, we don't know what we are up against. So we need to wait and assess the situation before we act.'

'This sounds like something Amarjyot would do,' Sharma said.

This asshole is still making it about him and Amarjyot Sir, Aryaman thought, running a hand through his salt-and-pepper hair.

'So, we wait for how long exactly?' Sharma asked.

'Monitor all chatter,' Aryaman said to Randheer. 'Look out for any keywords on the Internet. Video games, social-media sites. Anything. And of course, the physical entry points have to be under scrutiny.'

'Yes,' Sharma said. 'The needful will be done. But, Aryaman . . .'

'Yes, sir?'

'Are you certain about doing it this way?'

'Is there any other way?'

After a brief spell of silence, Sharma conceded.

'Well,' he said, smiling ever so slightly. 'At least you called me sir.'

Aryaman pulled out a cigarette and leaned forward. He knew he couldn't smoke in there, but he didn't care about insubordination anymore.

'We're not friends,' Aryaman said. 'We can never be. I'm here for my wife, for Amarjyot Sir and for my country. Not necessarily in that order.'

Aryaman stood up, walked out of the office and lit his cigarette.

16

Dubai

It wasn't the best hotel around, but it would certainly make do. Dubai had some of the most lavish places to stay at. But all Asra and Eymen wanted was a modest bed and some freshly cooked food, especially after the terrible journey that had made them seasick. They had successfully carried out most of their plan by transporting the weapon to India. But it wasn't over yet.

Asra's handler, Ashraf Asif, had personally taken charge of the consignment that held the vials. He was there to usher them to safety when the cargo ship arrived at the port. He didn't tell them how he would get the vials transferred, but he did tell them when and from where they would have to pick them up. That was all they needed to know, he assured them.

Asif told Asra about Lars Christiansen's death and the mishap in Turkey. She was scared. Someone was on to them, and they needed to act fast. Their plan had functioned like clockwork thus far. They just had to keep it that way now. Ashraf instructed Asra not to tell Eymen about this. Eymen was just working for them and did not need to be privy to such information. 'Besides,' Ashraf added, 'Eymen is committed to his cause to a fault. Let him believe we have the upper hand, unless we think we need to call off the mission altogether.'

They retired to their hotel (run by Pakistanis, unsurprisingly) later that evening. Asra and Eymen, between them, had smoked forty cigarettes since morning. In the room, they were mostly silent, unwilling to converse. They only spoke about work. But there was still one question that Asra wanted to ask. Why was Eymen this committed to the cause? He had never answered this question directly. Her boss probably knew why, but Asra didn't. She thought, *Do I need to know his motivations? Does it matter?*

Eymen lay slumped on the sofa with his eyes shut. From the bed, she looked at the awkward posture of his body, rolled up uncomfortably.

'I can take the couch,' she offered. He half-opened his eyes to look at her and smiled politely. That was the first time she had seen him do that.

'Come on, get on the bed. There's enough place for you, Eymen.'

'That's fine.'

'I insist.' She smiled back. 'I don't bite.'

Eymen stood up sluggishly and walked towards the bed. Asra was eyeing him invitingly. He got in and covered himself with a blanket, avoiding Asra's stare.

'Why are you so driven to do this, Eymen?'

He was silent.

'Destabilizing India is my duty,' she prodded him further. 'I'm doing this for myself, to rise through the ranks of the PIA.'

Eymen scratched the grey stubble on his bald head and fixed his eyes at the ceiling. She leaned in closer towards him, touching his shoulder delicately.

'But there's a feral madness in you. And I can't place it. Sure, my bosses have asked me to help you on this mission and I will. But you are willing to wear that vest yourself and detonate it? Why?'

'Is that why you called me to the bed?' he said. 'So you can try to get me to talk about my motives?'

She began to stroke his arm delicately. 'Is it working?'

'Only if you tell me, first, what your PIA handler took you aside to tell you. At the port. I saw you guys talking as I went to the washroom.'

She paused for a bit and then lay her head down on the pillow.

'Is it something to worry about,' he asked flatly. 'Is our plan still on? His body language was one of a worried man.'

'He didn't seem worried at all,' Asra said.

'Exactly,' Eymen resumed. 'He was portraying a false sense of confidence. I could see that about him.'

Asra didn't say anything.

'I just caught up on all the news too, Asra. It may have been a small article that could mean nothing, but I read about a police standoff with some criminals. And then I saw a clip too, filmed by locals. Lior's guard was in it.'

Asra sat up and drank some water. 'It's nothing to worry about. My boss assured me. But, if you must know . . .'

Eymen held his breath. A shadow of worry began to form on his face.

'Lior was arrested by Turkish officials.'

Eymen went into a state of shock, cursing out loudly and covering his face with his hands. He punched the bed hard.

'I knew it,' he said through gritted teeth. 'That son of a bitch had trouble written all over him. I don't even think he is arrested. He would sell his mother for the right price. He must have sold the information about our attack to the intelligence authorities!'

Eymen, almost red in the face, was now pacing around the room.

'We have reasons to believe he has been actually arrested,' Asra said. 'My boss is certain about that.'

'And how can he be so sure?'

Asra thought, *Maybe I should tell him. After all, the man is committed to his cause.*

'You have to tell me now, Asra. Or I go ahead with this attack by myself. As you rightly pointed out, I don't mind if I die in my mission.'

Asra got to her feet and walked up to Eymen. She put a hand on his shoulder and said, 'My boss spoke about an entity, much bigger than all of us combined, that is masterminding this attack.'

'So?' Eymen asked, fuming.

'So that entity has people everywhere,' Asra said. 'And when it wants things done, it sees them through till the end.'

Signs of exhaustion were visible on Eymen's face. He sat on the edge of the bed with a sigh, and Asra sat beside him.

'I don't give a fuck about any entity.' Eymen's voice had lowered. 'This plan will not stop. I won't let it stop. I have dreamed of the day I make India crumble.'

There was anger in his eyes but also vulnerability. She placed her hand on his thigh.

'Relax,' she said. 'It will be done. Now tell me your story?'

Eymen watched Asra's hand sliding up his thigh.

'Or do you want to tell me in a bit?' She smiled suggestively.

Asra had received very strict orders during her days at the PIA training camp about not using sex as a tool unless it was absolutely necessary to do so, or unless she was instructed to do so by those in charge. This rule especially came into effect when she was dealing with an asset. There was always a chance that the man, or even she, might form a romantic attachment, which was sure to jeopardize the plan. But this particular case, to her mind, was different. Besides, she had her own needs to fulfil. And she was sure Eymen had those needs too.

After having made love to her twice, Eymen lay spent on the bed. He had been surprisingly gentle with her. She was discovering something new about him every day. And now, she was about to discover the truth about him.

He looked at her naked body and then into her eyes.

'Believe it or not,' Eymen said. 'I was once a man of service myself. About six years ago.'

2011: Ibrahim Khalil, between Iraq and Turkey

Eymen, the head of security at the Ibrahim Khalil border crossing, stood upright in his Peshmerga uniform. The frontier, although an entry point into Iraq, was controlled by the Kurdistan Regional Government. The Peshmergas—the Kurdish word translates to 'those who face death'—were the military forces of the autonomous region of Iraqi Kurdistan. That morning, Eymen was expecting a peaceful protest at the border. He stood below the flag and kept his eye on the Kurdish protestors and on the medial personnel.

Eymen instructed some of his subordinates to walk over to the protesters and provide them with food and water. He knew his people, the Kurds, all too well. They were simple and straightforward, and they wanted to carve out their own territory, independent of both Iraq and Turkey. The Turks and the Iraqis, predictably, had a problem with this and acted with hostility towards the Kurds. Many casualties were left in the wake of the skirmishes fought over the question of Kurdistan. But Eymen understood that a cause was a cause, and that politics was politics.

He spotted an elderly couple at the edge of the crowd. As he drew closer, he recognized them instantly. They were his parents. He walked up to them. His father, wizened and grizzled, laid a loving hand on his head. His mother held a placard that read: 'WE ARE NOT IRAQI!' Many others held similar placards along with the Kurdish flag—the red, white and green tricolour with a golden sun at its centre.

Eymen's eyes were trained to detect things out of the ordinary. The minute he saw one protestor shouting out slogans with a gusto that seemed a touch exaggerated, he knew something was off.

Eymen excused himself from his parents and began to make his way towards this man, wading through the crowd. The suspect, however, was considerably far away. Eymen began to call out for him. But his voice was drowned by the crowd's sloganeering. And then, what Eymen saw frightened him beyond measure. The protestor had dropped small pouches on the ground— three pouches to be precise. He then broke away from the crowd and ran. Eymen set off after him.

The protestor was quick on his feet, but he was no match for Eymen. As he caught up with him, Eymen saw a detonator in the protestor's hand. He hurled the man to the ground with all his strength. And the protestor, without wasting any more time, clicked the detonator. Within seconds, the three pouches exploded, releasing a thick cloud of smoke and gas. The crowd went into a frenzy of panic, stampeding in all directions. Eymen thought of his parents. He wanted to run back and rescue them, but the man responsible for the attack lay on the ground before him, ready to dash away.

In a split second, he took the decision. He realized his men would begin to clear out the crowds as soon as possible. So he pummelled the protestor unconscious. He lifted him on his shoulder and ran towards his vehicle, throwing the protestor in the back of the car. Then he drove straight to an intelligence safe house nearby.

After subjecting the protestor to a few days of rigorous interrogation, Eymen discovered the truth. The gas he had detonated was sarin—a nerve agent that attacked the nervous system and caused excruciating and uncontrollable muscle contractions that made it difficult to breathe, eventually leading to death by asphyxiation. The reason the protestor gave them for the attack came as a surprise to Eymen and his men, and it was far removed from the politics of this part of the world. While the attacker was supposed to pass himself off as a Turkish man with anti-Kurdish ideals, the truth was substantially different. He was an Indian.

The attack, Eymen was told, was a diversionary tactic used by the Russians who wanted to draw attention to the region. They would, in the meanwhile, smuggle a nuclear warhead into Azerbaijan. Turkey was involved in several shadow wars with the KGB. But with India? They were supposed to be allies. And naturally, when this news reached them, the Indian authorities denied and condemned the attack, although they conceded that the assailant was probably an Indian. But for Eymen, things had become personal, and he was in no mood to go with the narrative that was being forced upon him. Henceforth, he would do what he felt was right in pursuing his vendetta.

Asra saw Eymen's eyes welling up. She handed him a bottle of water which he drained in one go.

'What happened to the Indian? Was India involved in the interrogation? Was he proven to be a mercenary or was India in the know?'

Eymen let out a dry laugh.

'I snapped his neck soon after he confessed. I knew he was politically motivated. Not a gun-for-hire, even though there was no proof to tie him to the Indian government. I was dismissed by my seniors. Let off easily, since they knew I was right. But I had to leave my motherland. And . . .'

'And?'

'My parents succumbed to the gas,' he said, choking up. 'The gas detonated by a fucking Indian. They died a painful death. Disintegrated before my eyes within days. And I will make the Indians go through what they made my parents and my people go through.'

Eymen held Asra firmly.

'I will carry out this attack. You leave if you have to. Tell your bosses I went rogue. I wasn't in your control. But nothing can stop me. I will do it their way. An eye for an eye . . .'

Asra's phone buzzed. She broke out of his embrace and saw a message from Ashraf Asif. Eymen watched her read it over the next few minutes. She looked at Eymen with half a smile.

'You don't have to do the attack. You don't have to die for their sins. This man will do it for us.'

She raised her phone in the air. There was a picture of Aryaman on the screen.

17

Covert IRW unit, Mumbai

Randheer, with Aryaman beside him, drove past a security checkpoint after flashing his ID card. They were visiting Avantika in a makeshift facility where she was attempting to produce batches of the antidote. So far they hadn't received any positive updates from her. In fact, the bad news had got them to drive to the facility. They had no idea what they were going to do exactly. Moral support perhaps. But the clock was ticking and even moral support wouldn't amount for much now.

Aryaman got out of the vehicle and entered the building that had a grey and drab façade. From the inside, however, the building seemed considerably sleek. Steel walls and wooden flooring adorned its large foyer. Randheer went towards the reinforced-steel door of the laboratory and presented his card to the security guard.

'By the way,' Randheer said with a slight chuckle. 'I told my men to be more careful about keeping an eye on your mother and child. Told them she sniffed the two of them out in no time.'

Aryaman shrugged in response.

'But they had a funny thing to say,' Randheer continued as they put on their hazmat suits. 'They said they never tailed her down any street on that particular day. So then I had to give them an earful for not doing their job.'

Aryaman knitted his brows. 'What if it was someone else? Ma couldn't have been wrong.'

'You're paranoid,' Randheer said. 'Anyway, they'll keep a constant eye on her now.'

'What if they know about her?' Aryaman said, his face showing signs of panic.

'Who's "they"?'

'These fucking terrorists,' Aryaman spat out. 'What if they identified me after Goa? Or Turkey?'

Randheer placed a hand on Aryaman's shoulder. Avantika was here, as was, surprisingly, Bipin Sharma, who was overseeing everything.

'I'm going to talk to my son,' Aryaman told Randheer.

They stepped in. When Aryaman greeted Sharma politely, he received a grouchy response and turned his attention to Avantika, who acknowledged him with a cursory nod. There were bottles of various chemicals placed next to her, as well as two dead rats in glass containers.

'Any luck?' Randheer asked her.

She pointed at the two dead rats and then at a small metal case. 'Trying another version of the formula,' she said. 'The one we had prepared earlier was slow to battle the virus. We can't use that. It will spread like wildfire, and no amount of quarantining will help if we don't have a formula that acts quickly.'

'How long does the previous formula take to work?'

She scratched her chin. 'A week, perhaps. I'm trying to reengineer it, so that it can start fighting the virus in a day, tops.'

Everyone's eyes were fixed on the steel container in which the more potent antidote was being prepared.

'Third time's a charm,' Randheer said.

'Well, let's hope.'

Avantika's hands were trembling as she filled a syringe with the colourless liquid. She walked over to a third rat that was seemingly comatose.

'The genetic and biological characteristics of rats closely resemble those of humans,' she said tiredly as she injected the fluid into the rat. 'This little guy is infected by the virus. If he wakes up, we have made the breakthrough.'

Aryaman glanced sideways at Sharma.

'It takes a while,' Sharma said in his flat tone. 'Step out for a smoke?'

'I don't smoke,' Aryaman said gruffly, his eyes settling back on the rat.

Sharma stood up and left the room. Randheer was trying to hold back his laughter. Aryaman first smirked at him, and then the two of them burst out laughing.

'The world is about to end and the two of you are giggling like schoolgirls,' Avantika said, partly exasperated and partly amused.

'Exactly why we're laughing,' Aryaman said. 'If the world is ending, might as well laugh. Or maybe you can stop it from ending since you started the whole process in the first place.'

He looked at the rat reacting to the antidote.

'Give it an hour,' Avantika said. 'Let's hope this works.'

The three of them took their seats in a corner. When Sharma re-entered the room after a few minutes, Aryaman turned to Avantika and asked her, in mock earnestness, 'Smoke?'

Randheer turned red in the face, trying to control his chuckle.

'Why not,' Avantika said.

They unzipped their hazmat suits and walked out of the facility. He lit a cigarette first for her and then one for himself.

'I'm sorry that you have to go through all this, Avantika. But only you can get us out of this.'

She blew out a cloud of smoke resignedly, her eyes meeting his.

'Well, if it hadn't been for you, I would've been dead by now,' she said. 'Either killed or committed suicide. I don't think I could cope with this by myself.'

Aryaman looked at his watch as Avantika placed a hand on his injured shoulder.

'Besides, I haven't seen someone go to this extent to protect his country. Aryaman, whether or not the attack happens, nobody can accuse you of not trying your best.'

Aryaman finished the cigarette and turned towards the facility.

'Thanks,' he said. 'But this antidote had better fucking work. Or this attack will kick-start World War Three.'

They walked back into the facility, where a horrified Randheer awaited them. Sharma rubbed the bridge of his nose nervously as he pointed at the rat.

'It hasn't worked,' he said. 'The rat's dead. We're fucked.'

Avantika examined the rat, which showed no signs of life. She burst into tears. The pressure was mounting and time wasn't on their side. Aryaman, too, had a lump in his throat.

'I can try again,' she said, sniffling. 'I can try again.'

'Sir,' Aryaman said to Sharma. 'Let her give this another shot. But I think we need to get back to the headquarters and rethink our strategy, taking into consideration that there is no effective antidote. The bomb cannot go off at any cost.'

Dehradun

'Is this happening because of Pakistan?' Aditya asked
his grandmother in his innocent, endearing way. 'Are
they doing this to us?'

Aarti looked a little taken aback at the suddenness
of the question. She had to answer carefully. Aditya was
at an age when perceptions are formed. Perceptions
that could last a lifetime.

'No,' she said. 'The Pakistani people want just
what we want: peace. And then there are people who
want to profit from war. Those are the people who are
doing this. They are not followers of any religion and
don't represent the country they are born in. They are
enemies of peace and harmony.'

Aditya nodded. Aarti prepared a hot chocolate for
him. They had closed the kitchen for the night and were
waiting for the last two customers to leave. After that
she would have to clean up and call it a night. She was
curious to know what Aryaman was up to after their last
call. He had sounded calm and composed. But still, he
was her son, and she knew something was worrying him
when he asked her whether she had once again spotted
anyone tailing her. She told him she hadn't and that he
was being paranoid. She decided to drop Randheer a
message, asking him to call whenever they got the chance.

She watched Aditya sipping his drink. Chor had
placed his head on Aditya's lap and was staring up at
him, wagging his tail.

'What are you thinking about, Aditya?'

'I didn't get a chance to know my dad well enough when Mom was alive,' he said. 'But now that he's here, I am hoping to become like him. Weird as he may be.'

Aarti smiled at him.

The two customers placed the money they owed for the meal on the table, waved her goodbye and left the cafeteria.

'Go clear up that table for me,' she instructed Aditya. 'Help me clean up. It's late.'

She looked at the clock: half past twelve. Aditya did as he was told. Meanwhile, Chor walked up to Aarti, who had just begun to pet him when she heard a scream.

It was Aditya. She looked up to see the two men, their faces covered, dragging the shrieking boy out of the cafeteria. Aarti picked up the sharpest knife within her reach and tried to get to them as quickly as her aged legs allowed. Chor was quicker. He sprang into action and ran to save Aditya, barking ferociously at the attackers.

Aarti confronted them and swiped her knife at the one holding Aditya. But the attackers were strong. A gash on the shoulder wasn't going to change anything. Chor sank his teeth into the other attacker's thigh. The man yelled in pain and kicked the dog aside. But Chor was unrelenting. He leapt at the attacker who held Aditya and bit into his shin.

The ruckus caused the elderly Arora couple to wake up and peep outside their window. They were stunned at what they saw.

'I hate to do this,' one of the attackers said, pulling out a pistol with a silencer attached to it. 'But I will kill this fucking dog and the rest of you.'

Aarti pulled Chor away and looked at the Aroras at their window.

'Go get those two who were watching us from the window,' one of the attackers ordered the other.

The man obediently limped towards that window, brandishing his weapon. Aditya was sobbing as his assailant yanked him by the hair. Aarti tried to stop Chor from barking, but she wasn't doing a very good job of it.

'Stop that fucking dog,' the man screamed.

There were sounds of two gunshots outside. Chor suddenly fell silent. Surmising the worst, Aarti thought that the Aroras had been shot dead. The window in their house opened and the other attacker motioned for his companion to come over.

'We can hold them in here,' he shouted. 'Quick.'

Aarti and Aditya were dragged into the other house. What Aarti saw relieved her. The elderly couple was alive, albeit trussed up on a chair each.

'It's okay,' the assailant said. 'Nobody gets hurt if we get what we want.'

The men turned towards Aarti.

'What is it that you want?' Mr Arora interrupted. 'Money? Jewellery? Take it all and leave.'

'Mr Arora,' the assailant turned to him. 'We thought you were an army guy. Did your bravery retire with you? Do you think we're here for jewellery of all things?'

Mr Arora wasn't surprised that they knew of his army background. Almost all of Dehradun knew about it.

'Then untie me and watch the soldier within me take over,' Mr Arora spat at him.

'Well,' the assailant shrugged. 'You should have shot me when you had the chance. Guess old age slows one's reflexes, doesn't it?'

Mrs Arora was trembling with fear.

'What is it that you want then?' Aarti asked.

The other man walked over to Aarti. 'We want you to call your son, Aryaman.'

18

Mumbai

A digital reconstruction of what Eymen and Asra looked like was sent across to all major intelligence and security agency heads, who were tasked with circulating it within their networks and keeping an eye out for anyone that matched the descriptions. All personnel were advised to be discreet.

Randheer had scoured for leads in the several tapes of potential suspects who could be the duo in disguise that the airport authorities had sent him. None of them really stood out. The manhunt was getting increasingly tense. Randheer, Aryaman and Sharma had deduced that the attack would happen within the next few days—considering that the weapon had, in all probability, made its way to India.

Ashraf Asif, Eymen and Asra had reconvened at a safe house in a seedy area of Byculla. Their big moment had almost arrived. Ashraf had taken charge of smuggling the weapon from Dubai into India. Even Asra didn't know how he had done it. He wanted no fuck-ups, and the fact that someone like him was directly involved made it clear to Asra just how much this mission meant to him. What she did not realize was that Ashraf himself had a superior to report to.

Ashraf locked his room in the safe house and got on a call via his secure laptop after dispensing instructions to Eymen and Asra. He made sure they'd left the house—on a task assigned by him—before he got on the call. Exactly after one sharp ring, the Scorpion came on.

'Aryaman's family is with my men,' Ashraf said. 'He doesn't know about it yet.'

The Scorpion was quick to respond. 'I am not in favour of last-minute improvisations such as these. But because it's Aryaman, I will make an exception.'

'Do you know him?'

'Rather well,' the Scorpion snorted. 'Aryaman was the bad child of the Indian intelligence community. In 2013, he was part of an Indian team that killed Maqsood Akram. The operation left almost the entire team dead. The old guy who was running the op committed suicide.'

'But has Aryaman done anything to you? Does he . . .'

'Nobody knows who I am, Ashraf. My organization has united able people like yourself to take over the world and change its map one step at a time. If you pull tomorrow's mission off, I will meet you.'

'I look forward to that,' Ashraf said gleefully. 'It will be an honour.'

'I will track the mayhem very closely,' the leader continued. 'Your laptop will have a rendezvous point set up as soon as you finish this. And together, we will move on to our next phase of expansion.'

Ashraf nodded assent.

'Now tell me,' the Scorpion continued. 'How do you intend to make Aryaman conduct the attack?'

Ashraf sat upright and lit a cigarette. 'If his family is being held at gunpoint, he will go to crazy lengths. His wife is dead. His mentor, whom he loved, killed himself, like you said. He doesn't really have anyone besides his mother and son.'

'But if you tell him that you have them captured, he will send someone to free them. And that still doesn't guarantee that he will carry out the attack. You need to bring him before you and give him the bomb yourself. He is not to be underestimated.'

Exhaling a cloud of smoke, Ashraf said, 'I have thought that through, sir. We will draw him to us.'

'How?'

'Eymen and Asra are on it as we speak.'

The *Indian Daily Report* newsroom was its usual self. Jyoti's death had shaken the staff to the core, but there was still news to report each day. Ehsaan's work had doubled. After his conversation with Aryaman and Randheer, he lived in constant fear that he was the next target. But it had to be done—the paper had to be kept running—for Jyoti. There was no other way.

On more than one evening, Ehsaan got piss drunk and attempted to call Randheer. He wanted to ask if the two men supposed to be protecting him were still on duty. But Randheer, who knew exactly why Ehsaan was trying to reach out, never answered his calls, reassuring him with coded text messages on WhatsApp. Something along the lines of, 'God is always watching us. So we must bow our heads down to him and pray whenever we are free.' The kind of stuff middle-aged housewives would forward on their WhatsApp groups first thing in the morning. Nonetheless, it served the purpose of calming Ehsaan down.

But on that evening, what Ehsaan didn't know was that along with God, two others were watching him. And these two were pretty much the opposite of God: where God created, they wanted to destroy.

They were Eymen and Asra, who had managed to spot the two agents protecting Ehsaan—ordinary-looking guys who would've ranked low in the intelligence system and were allotted basic tasks like surveilling people who weren't in any real danger.

But this is where the Indians would be wrong, Asra thought.

'You grab the journalist before he gets to the scooter,' she instructed Eymen. 'I will take care of the agents.'

Eymen raised an eyebrow at her. 'You sure? Should I do that instead?'

She shook her head resolutely. 'No, I've got this.'

As soon as Ehsaan stepped out of the office and started walking briskly towards his scooter, Eymen jumped out of the SUV he was in with Asra and charged towards him. Ehsaan froze. Everything happened all too quickly for him to understand that he was being abducted and not killed. The lane was relatively quiet, except for a couple of shocked onlookers who saw Eymen land a blow to Ehsaan's solar plexus. Ehsaan wheezed as he tried to cry out for help, but he was dragged along and forced into the SUV by Eymen.

Seeing this, the two agents sprang out of the shadows and rushed towards the car. Asra reversed the vehicle, rolled down the windows and with two quick but calculated shots, killed them instantly.

Ehsaan began to wail. He begged for a quick death. Eymen put a generous amount of duct tape on Ehsaan's mouth, and they drove to an abandoned mill complex, pulling over in one of the large factories.

Ashraf Asif, his sedan parked inside, was already waiting for them. There was a cruel smile on his face. Ehsaan was theirs. And soon, Aryaman would be theirs too. They were now in the penultimate phase of the attack.

Eymen tied Ehsaan to a steel chair. Ashraf leaned forward towards him and tugged the tape off his face. Ehsaan howled, begging them to either kill him or let him go.

'We will let you go,' Ashraf said. 'We don't want to hurt you. We just want your friend to visit us.'

'Friend?' Ehsaan looked at Eymen.

'Aryaman,' Ashraf resumed. 'Jyoti's husband. Bring him here and this ends for you. Here, take your phone and call him. Any funny business and a bullet ends this for you.'

Aryaman had been recovering from his injuries and drinking copiously in the bargain. His safe house smelled of cigarettes and alcohol. Avantika, who had spent hours at the lab facility, had still not made any breakthrough. She was pale as a sheet, ate very little and spoke even less. Her mind was always on the antidote. She was trying to catch spells of sleeping-pill-induced forty winks to power through.

The entire ordeal had taken a toll on Aryaman physically, even though mentally he was still in the game. His recent exchanges with Bipin Sharma had inspired in him a certain confidence that he would have the agency's support in taking down the terrorists once they had identified them.

'Randheer,' Aryaman said worriedly, after trying his mother's phone for the sixth time. 'Something's wrong. They aren't picking up.'

Randheer made a quick call to his men who were keeping an eye on Aarti and Aditya. They answered instantly.

'Is the family okay?'

'Sir,' Randheer's man replied. 'They haven't left the house. Everything's okay. No need to panic.'

Randheer put the call on speaker phone and asked the man to repeat his statement. Aryaman seemed relieved to hear it.

'Good,' Randheer spoke into the phone. 'Keep a close watch on them and continue to update me.'

Aryaman decided to wake Avantika up. He needed to drive back to the facility with her and get her to begin work again. He pushed open the door to her room and saw her curled up in a ball on the bed, her red-rimmed, watery eyes already open, watching him.

'Is it time to go?' she asked.

'Did you sleep?'

She shrugged and stared at the ground. Her voice lacked all strength. 'What if I fail, Aryaman?'

He sat beside her and placed his hand gently on her shoulder.

'You won't,' he said, gravely. 'You can't.'

She struggled to sit up and took a sip of water from the bottle he'd handed to her.

'Get ready,' Aryaman said and left the room. A little later, he saw Jyoti's phone buzzing on the table. He hurried to it, thinking it was his mother or son calling him. Instead, he saw a name he least expected to see at that moment: Ehsaan.

He showed the screen to Randheer, who said, 'Must be one of his paranoid calls.'

Aryaman answered and put him on speaker.

'Yes?'

'Aryaman,' Ehsaan's voice was unsteady. 'I will be sending you an address. I need you to come over. Alone. No Randheer, no cops, nobody.'

Aryaman stood with a sudden alertness. Randheer drew closer to listen in.

'Why? Did you find something?'

There was a momentary silence.

'Ye . . . Yes. Please. Alone. Immediately.'

The phone in Aryaman's hand vibrated, having received a GPS location pin.

'Alone, or else I'm dead, Aryaman. Please.'

The line went off. Aryaman turned to look at Randheer, who was calling Ehsaan's security cover. No answer. Aryaman rushed to the table and picked up the car keys.

'I need a gun,' he said to Randheer, who rushed to the drawer and tossed him a pistol. 'You take Avantika and head to the facility. I will see what the deal with Ehsaan is. Keep me posted.'

Aryaman pushed the door open and ran towards his car. Everything about Ehsaan's call had felt wrong to him.

He turned the ignition on and zoomed through the streets with complete disregard for traffic laws. His adrenaline was kicking in, and his heart was pounding against his chest. Ehsaan was a paranoid guy, no doubt. But through all his years in intelligence, Aryaman had learned to read people by observing the way they spoke in different situations. Ehsaan didn't sound like he was simply having a bad case of the nerves. It was much worse. There was someone around him—someone who was controlling what he said. And it was clear that Ehsaan's life was under immediate threat.

Aryaman pulled up at an abandoned mill. He stepped out of the car and scanned his surroundings, taking small steps forward, crunching dead leaves under his shoes. It felt like a trap. But if walking into this trap was the only way of getting to the bottom of this, so be it. He came to a large, rusty iron door and pushed it open.

In the flickering overhead light, he saw Ehsaan tied to a chair. And standing next to the hostage was a man with a pistol: Eymen Arsalan.

Aryaman wasn't surprised by this. In his mind, he had played out scenarios much worse than the one he was now faced with. He had imagined Ehsaan dead, with a bunch of men ready to take him out the minute he stepped in.

'So you are Aryaman,' Eymen said. 'Good to see you, my friend.'

Aryaman walked towards them. Ehsaan's face was purple with bruises and caked with blood. A cloth tied around his mouth prevented him from speaking. Eymen hadn't been gentle with him, but he had kept him alive, which was a sign that he wanted to negotiate, Aryaman thought. But whatever they wanted from him, they weren't going to get it, Aryaman was pretty sure of that too.

'Let him go,' he said. 'This is between us.'

'Nobody's going anywhere,' Eymen stated blankly. 'Until you do what we need you to.'

'And what is that?'

Eymen walked nonchalantly to his car, which was parked in the corner, and pulled out a vest with three vials attached to it.

'You do know what this is, don't you?'

Aryaman did. The bioweapon was ready to use, strapped on to a vest and fitted with a detonator.

'A poison. Your own country's creation.' Eymen smiled. 'And now it's going to be used on your own countrymen.'

Aryaman walked up to Ehsaan and undid the cloth around his mouth. Eymen offered no resistance to that move.

'There are two more of them,' Ehsaan spluttered. 'This is it, Aryaman. It's the end. We can't do anything about this.'

Ehsaan broke into tears. Aryaman placed a hand on his head to comfort him and then looked venomously at Eymen. 'Why did you call me here? You could have carried out the attack, and we would not have found you in time.'

Eymen laughed. 'That's true. But here's the thing. I would have had to sacrifice myself too.'

'Everyone needs to pay a price.' Aryaman smiled back at him.

'Yes,' Eymen said. 'Exactly. And you will have to pay the price.'

Aryaman charged at him and attempted to throw a punch at his face. But Eymen swerved to the side and hit Aryaman on the temple with the butt of his gun. Eymen landed another kick to Aryaman's gut. It was a powerful kick and would have shattered his rib had it been any higher. Aryaman dropped to the ground, but only for a second. He recovered and stood right up. He shoved Eymen against his car.

Eymen raised his hands in the air and said, 'You wouldn't want to waste time, Aryaman.'

Eymen took out his phone and offered it to Aryaman, who snatched at it. He wasn't prepared for what he saw. His mother, his son and the Aroras were facing the camera. Two large men, their faces covered, stood beside them. He saw tears running down his son's face. His mother, even though she tried not to show it, seemed scared. It was a live video feed. Aryaman flung the phone aside and launched a kick into Eymen's chest.

'Stop!' Ehsaan cried. 'Or they will kill your family.'

Aryaman was in a fit of rage. And then he broke down . . .

Eymen got to his feet, rubbing his chest. 'The price to pay is yours. Your family or the people of your city.'

Aryaman's mind had gone numb.

'You wear that vest tomorrow, at the 26/11 anniversary memorial,' Eymen said. 'And amid the crowd, you detonate it.'

'There is strict security. You will never be able to . . .'

'We have taken care of the security at the entrance,' Eymen said. 'It will be an easy entry for you. Wear the vest under a jacket. Step in among the thousands of people who are there to pay their respects. And detonate the bomb. Your family gets to live.'

Aryaman dropped to his knees, his head in his hands.

'Don't do this . . .' he said. 'Don't take their lives. They are innocent.'

Eymen clucked his tongue. 'None of that bullshit, Aryaman. Will you do it?'

Aryaman was silent. Eymen walked over to Ehsaan, grabbed his hand and wrenched his little finger out of joint. Ehsaan howled in pain.

'WILL YOU DO IT?' Eymen screamed at Aryaman.
Aryaman shook his head.

Eymen pressed his gun against Ehsaan's forehead.

'He dies. Your family dies. You die. And I do the
attack anyway.'

Aryaman's jaw was trembling as he said, 'Don't . . .'

Eymen's finger was on the trigger, ready to blow
Ehsaan's brains out.

'You can save a lot of people if you conduct the
attack,' Eymen continued. 'You couldn't save your
wife. But you can save your son and mother!'

Aryaman got to his feet, shaking with rage but
looking defeated. He saw the vest and closed his eyes.

'Answer me now. We don't have all day. If you do
this, I spare all those who matter to you.'

There were tears in Aryaman's eyes as he said, 'I'll
do it. I'll conduct the attack.'

19

Mumbai

The Gateway of India was beautifully illuminated in honour of the victims of that fateful night of 26 November 2008. It had now been over a decade since the day those ten Lashkar-e-Taiba terrorists swarmed in and carried out a series of attacks that brought the city to its knees. The coordinated massacre had lasted about four days, taking at least 170 lives and leaving some 300 injured. The city had been under siege, but the residents began to pick up the broken pieces soon after, resuming their everyday lives with their indomitable spirit.

The city was now paying homage to the martyrs of 26/11. Around 200 people had gathered at the Gateway of India, and the number was increasing with every passing minute. A popular actor had just taken to the stage and was addressing the crowd. It was a sombre moment for everyone present—some were reduced to tears as they lit their candles and uttered their prayers. Little did they know that there were plans for an unprecedented attack to be carried out that very night by a patriot who had repeatedly put his life on the line for his country.

The Indian flag fluttered proudly in the wind. People bowed their heads in respect. The actor's voice from the stage broke the two-minute silence. Aryaman, still sore from his recent confrontation with Eymen, limped towards the metal detector frames that were manned by police personnel, who stood between him and the swelling crowd that he was going to infect with a deadly virus.

Aryaman's eyes met those of a policeman. They nodded to each other, and Aryaman put on his hoodie. The policeman stepped back and turned off the metal detector as Aryaman went through. Aryaman read the policeman's name as he moved past: Sanjay Rane.

Although he had switched off the security system to allow Aryaman to pass, Rane went slightly against Eymen's plan and frisked Aryaman when he saw that a fellow constable was casually looking over at him. Aryaman felt Rane's hand go over the concealed vest. The frisking done, Rane cleared Aryaman and gently pushed him in towards the venue.

Aryaman moved past the crowd, reluctantly walking towards the centre, where he was supposed to detonate the bioweapon. His unsure steps were being watched through a sniper scope by Eymen, who had perched himself atop a nearby terrace.

Eymen's instructions could be clearly heard through the earpiece that Aryaman was wearing: 'Any funny business and a bullet ends you on the spot. And I don't have to tell you what happens to your family after that.'

Aryaman didn't bother responding. He was going to do it. There were no two ways about that. He stepped on a poster that had the faces of the deceased printed on it with the words 'Gone But Not Forgotten', and he pushed past a group of children as he reached the centre.

A middle-aged woman looked at him disapprovingly. She saw his bruised face, his glassy eyes, his salt-and-pepper stubble and his dishevelled, greying hair. And then she witnessed something she couldn't decipher until it was too late. She watched him raise the detonator in his trembling right hand, drop to his knees and press the button. She heard a crack and saw fumes emanating from the man's torso. Fumes that turned to thick and pungent smoke. She cried out, but it was too late. The damage had been done. Tears ran down Aryaman's face. He had set the attack in motion.

There was mayhem—the kind Aryaman had rarely witnessed. People began to scream and run haphazardly. The actor, who until a few moments ago had been talking about how Mumbai had risen like a phoenix from the ashes after the 26/11 attacks, was now being whisked away by security personnel into an armoured car. Aryaman was jostled and pushed to the ground by the frenzied crowd. He lay on his back as smoke emanated from the weapon attached to his body.

A security team of four, all in hazmat suits, rushed towards him. They handcuffed and dragged him along the ground towards an armoured vehicle. Eymen, from his vantage point, alerted Asra, who was keeping a watch on Ehsaan.

'The job's done,' Eymen said. He had Aryaman in the crosshairs of his sniper rifle.

Asra's voice crackled through his earpiece. 'Good. Shoot him dead.'

'No,' Eymen said. 'That defeats the purpose of having him do it. He must seem like a lone wolf.'

'That's what I told Ashraf,' Asra said, a tinge of worry in her voice. 'But this is a last-minute development. Ashraf instructed us to kill him after he sets the virus off. Said something about Aryaman being a major hindrance if he is alive. He didn't say more but it seemed personal.'

'But . . .' Eymen seemed to hesitate.

'Do it, Eymen! Ashraf is waiting at the exit point!'

Eymen pulled the trigger . . .

Aryaman felt the bullet hit him in the chest. His whole body recoiled in pain.

The guards spoke into their walkie-talkies and alerted their cohorts, sending them in search of the sniper.

The sniper, however, had by now donned a different disguise. Dressed as a pizza delivery-boy, Eymen was already out of the building, on his bike, en route to the rendezvous point decided by Ashraf. He called Asra again.

'On my way to Ashraf. See you there. Aryaman's dead.'

Asra broke the news to Ehsaan, who had already accepted defeat. He knew there was no point waiting for a miracle. His fate had been sealed the minute Jyoti was killed.

'How's this for news, Mr Journalist.' Asra smiled. '"Indian Spy Turned Terrorist Conducts Deadly Bioterror Attack on His Country"; or: "Lone Wolf Turns Traitor". Hell, I could do this all day.'

Ehsaan spat blood at her. 'You will pay for this.'

Asra smirked and kneeled next to him. 'How? I would really like to know. Aryaman is dead. His wife is dead. Soon, the virus will spread through the city and then across the country. Everyone here is going to be dead. How will I pay for this?'

Ehsaan closed his tear-filled eyes.

'Oh,' she continued. 'I almost forgot. Aryaman's kid and mother are going to die too. He carried out the attack and bought them just a few more days. The virus will reach them at some point, I believe. What a sad end for your friend Jyoti and her family. Her husband is always going to go down as the man who attacked his country. Not one who laid down his life for it.'

Asra got to her feet and looked at her watch.

'Anyway,' she sighed. 'It was nice knowing you.'

Ehsaan saw her raise her pistol to his temple. He shut his eyes and heard the gunshot.

A moment later, Ehsaan, his eyes tightly shut, realized he was still alive. He opened his eyes and saw that Asra's pistol was on the floor and a stream of blood was gushing out of her hand.

Randheer was running towards her, firing away. She looked for cover, rushed towards the electricity meter, turned off the lights in the warehouse and, using the darkness to her advantage, made her way to her vehicle parked outside. Randheer couldn't find her. In any case, his first instinct was to run to Ehsaan.

'They . . . They killed Aryaman,' Ehsaan said as Randheer untied him.

Randheer, still on the lookout for Asra, didn't acknowledge him. And Asra had already driven off, her car kicking up a cloud of dust.

'There is backup arriving for you,' Randheer told Ehsaan, before hopping on to his motorbike and setting off after Asra.

As Randheer sped to catch up with Asra, he put on his earpiece and called his men in Dehradun. At that point, Asra's vehicle swerved violently—it hit a biker and sent him flying into a wall. It was a serious crash, but for Randheer, who thought that the biker would survive in all probability, catching Asra was the priority.

Randheer's men in Dehradun had received their orders, but they hadn't yet responded. Randheer began to panic. He sped through the streets of Mumbai. His friend's family was in danger, and it seemed like he had slipped up. He needed his men to save Aryaman's family, or else he would never forgive himself.

Dehradun

The two kidnappers had taken their masks off. Their grimy, bearded faces were exactly what Aarti had imagined them to be like. But they were a lot younger than she had expected. They were getting their instructions from Ashraf Asif, and they drew perverse pleasure from turning on the television and showing Aryaman's family the news as it played out. Aryaman's face was plastered over all the news channels, with the word 'terrorist' below it.

One of the news anchors yelled out an account of how the 'terrorist' was instantly shot dead by the police before he could conduct his second attack, which he apparently wanted to.

'That cannot be my son,' Aarti said, choking up. 'It can't. He can't . . . He can't do something as despicable as this.'

Aditya's face was red, and his eyes were swollen from all the crying. 'I want to . . . I want to die too.'

Aarti looked helplessly at her grandson. One of the kidnappers walked over to him and said with a grin, 'You will.'

The next moment, the door burst open. It was all over in a flash. Randheer's men were quick to act. A swift volley of bullets ended the kidnappers' lives in no time. Aarti, Aditya and the Aroras all screamed when they saw the blood, bits of bones and brains splattered all over the walls. Chor, who had been tied up, began to bark loudly.

'We're with Randheer,' one of the men clarified as he untied the hostages. 'Come on, we will drive you to a safe place. Sorry we didn't make it earlier.'

Mrs Arora had fainted. Aditya was taken away to be cleaned. There was blood—of the kidnappers—on his cartoon-print T-shirt. Aarti watched the dead bodies in stoic silence.

'Ma'am?'

One of Randheer's men was offering her water. She thanked him and emptied the bottle.

'They killed my son,' she said.

Randheer's men said nothing. One of them picked up the phone and called Randheer. No answer. He left a voice message: 'We have the family with us. Safe and secure.'

Mumbai

Asra pulled up outside the Mumbai Central train station and dashed in. Randheer followed her and began looking for her in what could easily have been one of the world's most crowded settings.

Asra had put her burqa on and was marching hurriedly towards the ladies' compartment of a train bound for Gujarat. She checked her phone for a message from Eymen, who was on the train, as Ashraf had planned. Ashraf himself was already on a plane to Gujarat; he would be waiting for them there, arranging their passage out of India. His plan wasn't the best, but it was the most feasible: an exit route via the sea, from the port of Gujarat.

As he ran through the swarm of people, Randheer's eyes chanced upon a trail of blood on the floor. It led towards the Gujarat-bound train that had just started moving. He decided to take the chance and sprinted after the moving train, jumping on board.

He pressed a button on his earpiece, made a call to
Bipin Sharma and began to move cautiously through
the juddering compartments.

'Sir,' he said. 'I'm on a train going towards Gujarat.
The assailants are on board, I believe. I think they
are going to leave the country via the Gujarat port. I
suggest you alert those security agencies.'

'I will make sure they don't get that far,' Sharma
said.

The armoured vehicle carrying Aryaman was speeding
towards the Mumbai safe house that Bipin Sharma had
arranged for the operation. The plan was outrageous,
but so far it had worked. Aryaman's 'death' had never
been a part of it, but they had taken it in their stride and
improvised. It was all for the best, Aryaman thought.

He sat up in the vehicle with the help of the
policemen. The one who was at the security gate of
the memorial event, Sanjay Rane, was also here. He
held up the vials that contained the actual bioweapon.
Aryaman pulled his bulletproof vest off and saw the
slug lodged in it with a wry smile.

'Sir,' the cop driving the vehicle said, pointing at
his GPS navigator. 'We have got a new location from
Randheer Sir. We have been instructed to go down that
route.'

Aryaman leaned forward and watched the blip that indicated Randheer's location.

'Hurry,' he said. 'It's a moving train!'

The cop nodded. 'We will have to follow it by getting on the tracks. There's a railway yard up ahead. I will take the vehicle through that.'

Aryaman gave him the go-ahead. The other cops, who weren't in on the plan, looked astounded. The car travelled at great speed towards the train.

'Sir,' one of the cops addressed Aryaman. 'So the gas that you set off there wasn't the virus?'

Aryaman sighed. He looked at Sanjay Rane, who took this as his cue to offer an answer.

'Basically,' Rane said, 'there was a lady who planned this attack. She tried to bribe me to allow Aryaman Sir into the venue and to overlook the fact that he had the vest attached to him. I agreed and took the money. But I reported it to my seniors immediately, who then put me on to a certain Randheer Sir. Randheer Sir told me to let Aryaman Sir through but discreetly pass on to him the vials with a harmless liquid. This was part of their larger plan to nab the terrorists. When he came up to me, we exchanged the vials, so he could detonate the right ones.'

'I had a bug on me,' Aryaman said. 'I wore it when I went to meet this Eymen guy, so that Randheer and Mr Sharma could listen in and know my every move. That enabled them to arrange for the other vials in the nick of time. So the gas that we detonated isn't really harmful, but the terrorists think their job is done. And that I'm dead. They'll be in for a surprise, for sure.'

Aryaman picked up a carrying case and placed the vials of the actual virus into it. When he locked it, he felt a sense of relief. He had been updated by Sharma about his family's safety too. Now all that was left to do was to catch the bastards behind this and bring them to book.

'Sir,' the driver turned to Aryaman. 'We have the train in sight. Hold on, it's going to be a bumpy ride!'

Aryaman made a call to Randheer. After the third ring, he answered. His voice was low, as he was carefully scanning the passengers, hoping to find Eymen and Asra.

'Yes?'

'We are catching up with the train, Randheer. Why don't you make it stop? There's a railway yard up ahead. We will evacuate the civilians and find Asra and Eymen.'

'Sounds like a plan,' Randheer said and proceeded towards the train driver's cabin. 'Close in once I slow the train down.'

Aryaman loaded his pistol and readied himself for what was to follow.

The train came to a halt. The passengers peered through their windows to see what was happening. Aryaman and the policemen got out of their vehicle.

'Get the civilians out of here,' Aryaman said to the cops. 'Get them out of the premises. We can't risk them being caught in the crossfire between us and the terrorists.'

Aryaman tiptoed towards the train. He saw Randheer and motioned for him to enter from up ahead. The cops began to evacuate the passengers. But Eymen and Asra were nowhere to be seen.

'Shoot at sight,' Aryaman said. 'No point taking them prisoners.'

Aryaman and Randheer communicated through their earpieces as they searched the train. The cops had cleared out most of the civilians, many of whom were noisy and cranky and cursed the 'government'.

'No,' Randheer responded to Aryaman's order. 'We must bring them in if we can. Don't make this personal yet, Aryaman. I know they almost killed your family and you. But the intelligence we could extract out of them is invaluable.'

Suddenly, all the lights on the train went out.

'Fuck,' Aryaman said. 'That must be them!'

A volley of bullets was sprayed towards Randheer. He dropped to the ground and rolled out of the train. He didn't know whether it was Eymen or Asra, but he was pretty certain that going in blind would lead to death.

On hearing the gunshots, Aryaman climbed to the top of a carriage to get a better view. He saw that the policemen were having a tough time keeping the crowd calm, but they seemed in control.

Randheer spotted Asra jumping out of the train and rushing towards the perimeter wall. He pursued her, vaulting over the wall after her and leaping across the rooftops of some rickety sheds.

Back in the yard, Aryaman saw Eymen creeping towards the police vehicle. But before Aryaman could alert anyone, Eymen pulled his gun out and shot the driver dead. Aryaman yelled in horror.

Eymen pulled the body out of the car and got into the driver's seat. He set off in the direction Asra had gone in. Aryaman leapt towards the roof of the car and landed on its top. Eymen started swerving the car to propel Aryaman off the roof. But Aryaman held on tight, straining every sinew in his arms. Finally, Aryaman saw his chance and opened the door. He swung into the car, landing a kick on Eymen's jaw.

The vehicle careered out of control and rammed into a parked train carriage. Shards of glass and metal flew through the car after the collision, injuring both Eymen and Aryaman. A sharp metal rod had pierced Aryaman's thigh. He bellowed in pain. But Eymen had suffered only minor cuts and gashes from the broken glass.

Aryaman hobbled out and climbed into the back of the armoured vehicle. Eymen followed him and kicked the rod sticking out of Aryaman's thigh, making him growl in agony.

Aryaman moved away from Eymen and, standing on one leg, tugged the rod out of his thigh. Eymen closed the door of the vehicle.

'Still got fight left in you, Aryaman?'

Eymen slammed him against the metal wall. 'By turning up here, you have infected all the civilians in that train. And me, too. But I don't care. I will kill you before I die. Besides, that pretty girl will hand me the antidote once you aren't around to protect her.'

Eymen began to strangle Aryaman, who spluttered and grinned until Eymen released his hold. Aryaman fell to his knees and picked up the case with the vials containing the virus.

'The real gas was never detonated.' Aryaman smiled, holding up the vials.

Eymen was stunned.

'We pulled wool over your eyes,' Aryaman said, his face soaked in blood. 'All that you did was in vain. That policeman you shot is our only real casualty. And for his death, I will make you pay.'

Aryaman smashed the rod on Eymen's temple.

'Maybe if you had conducted the attack yourself, you might have pulled this off. But you chickened out. And that's where you failed,' Aryaman spat out.

He began to pummel Eymen mercilessly. Doubling up to save himself, Eymen managed to wriggle free of Aryaman's grip at one point and got his hand on one of the vials.

'I will take you with me, Aryaman,' he said, smashing the vial against the door panel.

The vial cracked open and there was smoke as soon as the liquid came in contact with the air. Eymen was already on the verge of fainting.

Aryaman grabbed the hazmat suit he had worn earlier and kicked the door open. Though Eymen tried to grapple with him and hold him in, Aryaman managed to escape, slamming the door shut on Eymen.

Coughing hoarsely, Aryaman staggered towards the sheds.

At a distance, he saw a bunch of cops. By now, he had the hazmat suit on. It was stained with his blood. With much difficulty, he began to hobble towards the cops. Then he fell to his knees and crawled towards them. He saw Asra's lifeless body on the ground. But he wasn't prepared for what he saw when the cops moved out of his way and helped him up.

Randheer was dead. A bullet through his forehead.

Aryaman couldn't hold back tears. Besides him, Randheer had been the only surviving member of the Phoenix 5. He cried uncontrollably, holding his friend's hand. The cops stood away. Sharma arrived at the scene and watched on, silently, with tearful eyes.

'I'm sorry,' he muttered. 'I . . . I'm sorry.'

Aryaman passed out. The virus was doing its job.

20

Five weeks later . . .

It felt like he was back to where he didn't belong. The dreaded Quarry in Lakshadweep. He didn't have the strength to open his eyes. He felt hollow, almost as though his insides were non-existent. His muscles didn't comply, despite his greatest efforts to move them. This is what death felt like, he thought. But he wasn't quite dead yet. Maybe—another thought occurred—he should have been dead. End this madness once and for all. His wife, his mentor, his friends . . . All of them . . . Randheer too . . . All dead. And he was here, stuck in a limbo, trying to fight his way out.

'He's awake.'

Aryaman heard a woman's voice. It was Avantika.

He used every last ounce of his strength to lift his head from the pillow and open his eyes. Avantika stood alert before him, almost leaning in, her hands

pressed against a sheet of toughened glass. Aryaman
looked around. He was in a glass chamber. On his left,
a couple of feet away and in an identical chamber, was
Eymen Arsalan. Aryaman had needles sticking into
his arms, feeding the antidote into his bloodstream
through an intravenous drip.

Eymen was awake as well. He stared at the ceiling
listlessly, and his body was motionless save for his
chest's continual and irregular heaving.

'Aryaman,' Avantika said. 'You were exposed to
the virus. The antidote has taken a while to kick in,
but your body is showing signs of rapid recovery.'

'How long has it been?'

'Five weeks.'

Aryaman saw Bipin Sharma enter the room with
Aditya and Aarti. After making an attempt to sit up,
Aryaman fell back on his bed. When he saw his mother
and son weeping, his eyes began to well up. But he had
no time for emotions right now. He turned to Eymen.

'Why is that bastard still alive?' The question was
directed at Sharma. 'What happened to Randheer?'
Aryaman asked agitatedly.

'He had set off after Asra, the other operative,'
Sharma said. 'Asra had climbed on top of the roof of a
shed and was running along to find a safe spot to land
at. Randheer chased her. She shot him in the stomach
and he began to lose blood rapidly. He caught up with
her and emptied his cartridge at her. But before he
could make another move, she got a final, clean shot

at him. And then they both fell to the ground, where you saw them. We arrived at the scene too late to help.'

Aryaman was writhing in pain, letting out short, helpless sobs. He then heard a chuckle. Eymen was looking at the ceiling, grinning away. Aryaman jumped out of his bed, knocking down the drip stand, and moved towards Eymen's chamber with animal ferocity. But he soon realized that he was locked in his own cage, powerless to cause any harm to Eymen.

Aryaman noticed Eymen's bloodshot eyes and twisted smile. He noticed the similarities between Eymen's skin and his own. They had both gone completely pale, and their veins, purple and varicose, showed all over their bodies. They looked skeletal— like shadows of their normal selves.

'Open this door,' Aryaman growled to nobody in particular. 'I am going to end this son of a bitch once and for all.'

Sharma gestured for Aarti, Avantika and Aditya to leave. He waited until they were out and said, 'We retrieved Asra's phone. She was working for Pakistani intelligence and her handler was Ashraf Asif. Well-known in our circles. Wily old fox. But here's the thing: there is a mention of a location Asif, Eymen and Asra were supposed to go to after the attack was conducted. They chatted about meeting someone they referred to as the Scorpion.'

Aryaman processed the information.

'We have kept Eymen alive so that we could find out where this meeting was supposed to happen.'

'Fuck that,' Aryaman said and broke into a violent bout of coughs. 'Let's just kill him and find Asif some other way.'

'That's what I wanted to talk to you about, Aryaman,' Sharma said with an air of dejection. 'He has offered a deal. That we don't kill him and he tells us where Asra was headed.'

'He could be playing us,' Aryaman said. 'Set us on a wild goose chase. Or into a trap. How can we trust anything he says? He was planning to be a suicide bomber himself before this. He doesn't care if he dies!'

'And then he chickened out and left you to do the job, Aryaman. He's a coward bargaining for his life. In the end, all of them are exactly that. Cowards.'

Eymen didn't seem to move, but he could hear the entire conversation.

'If he knows where Asif Ashraf is headed, we can trace the Scorpion,' Sharma continued. 'It's worth a try.'

Aryaman let out a sigh and shook his head. 'Does the country know that the attack was not real?'

'Not yet,' Sharma said. 'We are feeding information to the media that we want put out. We've said that the virus hasn't been spread beyond a two-kilometre radius, and that we have secured everyone at a facility. It's inconvenient for them, but it will be short-lived, and they will be okay once this is all over. We are setting up bogus vaccination camps and quarantine procedures. We need Asif and this Scorpion bastard to believe their attack has been successful before we nail them.'

Aryaman knocked on the glass to get Eymen's attention. And Eymen, with great effort, turned to look at him. He seemed feeble, and his wounds from their fight at the railway yard were still raw.

'Do you know why you are lying there shrivelled up like a prune?'

Eymen said nothing.

'Because you did not have the courage to see the attack through. Had you not bailed on your plans and had you conducted the attack yourself, our country would have been in the midst of mayhem. Even if you wouldn't have lived to see it, your objective would have been complete.'

Aryaman got to his feet, shaking but trying to steady himself. Eymen looked on with a blank expression on his face.

'Left to me, I would tear through this wall and finish you off. But that's not the right thing to do, especially since the lives of many more are at stake if Asif Ashraf and the Scorpion are around. So tell us where they are . . .'

Aryaman's voice trailed off.

'. . . and I let you live,' Sharma completed his sentence. 'We continue to administer the antidote to you

until we decide what legal procedure we take with you.
But I ensure you, we take the death penalty off the table.'

Eymen closed his eyes. Maybe death was an
easier way out, he thought. Why be at the mercy of
these Indians? But then . . . Defecting to their side
would still guarantee him a life. And at that moment,
life was all he wanted. He wanted to live. He was
certain of that. They could call him a coward if they
wanted.

'If I tell you,' Eymen said, 'you promise you won't
kill me?'

Aryaman didn't respond.

'I want something in return for you to make good
on that promise,' Eymen continued. 'I want a lawyer
in the room. A witness and someone from my country.
And it has to be taped.'

Aryaman let out a short, derisive laugh.

'Agreed,' Sharma said. 'In two days, when you
can both leave the chamber, we go through with this
procedure.'

Eymen glared at Aryaman defiantly.

'Guess you'll have to live with the fact that I am
being spared for the greater good.'

Aryaman sat on the edge of his bed, trembling, a
volcano of rage about to erupt in him . . . But he said
nothing.

Two days later . . .

Aryaman was feeling much better. Avantika had declared him fit and helped him out of the chamber. She then drove him out of the secure premises.

'This has been a nightmare,' she said. 'But, is it all done, Aryaman?'

'It's never done, Avantika.'

'I meant, for you.'

There was genuine concern on her face. Aryaman looked at her and then out of the window.

'I never get to decide that myself.'

He saw a pack of cigarettes near the gear knob. When he picked it up, Avantika clucked her tongue and gestured for him to put it back. 'You're just about fine to be able to function normally,' she asserted. 'Definitely not fine enough to smoke though.'

Aryaman tossed the box back in its place. The car stopped outside a small temple. Avantika stepped out and led Aryaman to Aarti and Aditya, who had been waiting for them.

Aryaman embraced his mother and son. 'I'm sorry you had to face all that.'

'Don't be,' Aditya said.

'You have weathered greater storms,' Aarti said, running her fingers through Aryaman's hair.

They entered the temple for the prayer service that was being held here for Randheer. Walking past the mourners, they sat beside a smiling picture of Randheer. Aryaman had tears in his eyes.

The priest started chanting a prayer in Sanskrit. 'This is all because of me,' Aryaman said under his breath, and Avantika heard him.

'You need to stop blaming yourself, Aryaman. This isn't your cross to bear.'

'He had nobody,' Aryaman said. 'An orphan. Amarjyot Sir trained him to be the able agent he became. But he loved us intensely. His longing to be able to call someone his own was what made him join this mission. He had no stake in it.'

Aryaman stared at Randheer's jovial face in the photograph.

'Randheer laid his life down for his friend and for his country,' Avantika continued. 'You do what you do for a larger cause, don't you?'

Aryaman turned to Avantika.

'So make the most of what you have,' Avantika said, placing her hand on his. 'There are people who care for you.' As she said this her gaze shifted to Aditya and Aarti.

'I've heard there's a little dog who has joined your family. I'm sure he'll love you too.'

Aryaman smiled. He held Avantika's hand tightly, and they looked into each other's tear-filled eyes.

'You have been extremely brave through this,' he said. 'You deserve some rest. Would you like to . . .'

She peered at him in anticipation. 'Would I like to what?'

'You can fly down to Dehradun with my family,' he said. 'I'd like you to get some time away from all of this. And then, maybe when it is all done, we can meet again . . . This time, like two normal people.'

'I would like that,' said Avantika, smiling gently.

Aryaman saw Bipin Sharma's official sedan pull over outside the temple and went over to receive him. 'Well, you're early.'

Sharma shrugged. 'Still not done with your quips, are you?'

Sharma handed over a file to Aryaman, who opened it and began to read the documents forthwith.

'Eymen spilled the beans,' Sharma said. 'Told us everything we needed to know. Most of it was stale information we—you—had gathered along the way. But there is one crucial thing that . . .'

Aryaman had finished reading the transcript. He shut the file and handed it back to Sharma. 'So Asif and the Scorpion are meeting this week in Thailand?'

'Seems like it,' Sharma said, lighting a cigarette, which Aryaman eyed longingly.

'And are we keeping our promise? Can we kill him now that he has told us what we needed to know.'

Sharma didn't answer. 'Do you want to go to Thailand and fish them out?'

Aryaman closed his eyes. He couldn't get the image of Randheer's lifeless body out of his mind. He had to complete this. This chapter that had started with Jyoti's death and ended with Randheer's. He had to do this for the sake of his mentor, Amarjyot.

'I will,' Aryaman said. 'I will end this.'

'Good,' Sharma said. 'Once you finish it off, we kill Eymen too.'

Aryaman nodded. 'I need you to put out reports that reach Ashraf, saying that I have broken out of custody, that I am a fugitive. I need him to live with that looming fear.'

'By the way, we will require a codename,' Sharma said, placing a hand on Aryaman's shoulder. And I have one in mind.'

'What is it?'

'Of the five, you are the one survivor,' he said. 'So we should go with the Phoenix.'

Aryaman smiled. 'Cheesy, but I like it.'

Phuket, Thailand

Ashraf Asif was extremely pleased with himself. And rightly so. He had conducted one of the biggest attacks on enemy soil using one of their own citizens. He couldn't call it entirely his brainchild, since the Scorpion was pulling the strings from the shadows and helping him with resources that the PIA wouldn't readily sanction. But it was done. The PIA was pleased beyond measure.

They viewed Asra's death as collateral damage. There always was some, and that didn't irk them too much. Definitely not to the extent of dampening their spirits. Mumbai had not yet recovered from the attack, and the operations at the antidote vaccination camps were predictably chaotic for a city that had long burst at the seams in terms of the population.

Ashraf stopped before a beautifully constructed Buddhist temple and watched a few monks talking to each other jovially. Walking through the colourful market on Thalang Road, he thought about what lay ahead of him. The PIA was set to promote him to the top post in the coming years. And whatever shortcomings they might have in the money department, the Scorpion would more than readily compensate him for the mission.

His future seemed secure. He would be among the top brass of the Pakistani intelligence, and he was definitely not going to come cheap. He was loyal to his country, but he held money in a higher regard. That's why he had joined hands with the Scorpion in the first place. He would stack away the money in his offshore account, but he would never betray his country.

The Scorpion was all set to meet him. And that could only mean greater things were in store for him. Ashraf wasn't sure what the Scorpion's ultimate motive was. But today he was going to unearth that answer too. He needed to know who it was that the Scorpion was in cahoots with. It was about time.

Having been a spy for so many years, Ashraf knew when he was being tailed. He looked in the mirrors at stalls selling cheap sunglasses to see if anyone was following him.

But Aryaman himself was no rookie. He knew Ashraf would be less wary of those walking in front of him, especially in a crowd as dense as this. Aryaman used the same tools—mirrors at stalls and on bikes—to monitor Ashraf's movements. Finally, Ashraf entered a run-of-the-mill hotel; it wasn't the one he was staying at.

Aryaman examined the property. He needed to enter through another gate. Walking in right after Ashraf would raise suspicions. Aryaman went into a narrow bylane and arrived at the back of the hotel. He scaled the wall and saw a bellboy, who stood near the back door, smoking in silence.

'I'm going in,' Aryaman spoke into his earpiece. He jumped into the backyard, and just then the bellboy, startled by his presence, turned to run back inside. Aryaman pointed his gun at the bellboy and put his finger to his lips.

'Don't run,' he said. 'I just need your uniform.'

The boy was trembling all over but did as he was told, taking off his clothes.

'Thanks. And sorry for what I am about to do to you. But you will wake up in about an hour.'

Aryaman hit him on the temple with the back of his gun. The bellboy lost consciousness and slumped to the ground. Aryaman dragged him to the large trash container, opened its lid, and saw entrails of fish and prawn shells scattered among bulging bags of trash. His face contorted at the stench as he dropped the boy into the bin. He left its lid ajar, so that the boy wouldn't suffocate.

Now dressed as a bellboy, Aryaman entered through the back door with an employee's key card and walked quickly towards the reception, keeping his head down. He spotted Ashraf climbing the stairs, already two storeys up. A guest at the front desk snapped her fingers at a trolley full of suitcases, indicating that Aryaman take them to the room. He took the trolley and followed her into an elevator. Aryaman pressed all the buttons from the third floor up, so he could get a visual on Ashraf.

The elevator stopped at every floor. The woman was beginning to seem irritated, but Aryaman ignored her and watched out for Ashraf. Finally, he spotted him on the sixth floor. The woman wanted her luggage taken to a room on the eighth floor. He turned to her, snapped his fingers and pointed at the luggage.

'You're gonna have to take it yourself,' he said and stepped out. Ashraf had entered the room at the end of the corridor, locking the door behind him.

Aryaman spoke into his earpiece. 'Sixth floor. Going in.'

He tiptoed towards the door. His gun was at the ready, and he was about to break in when the door swung open. It was Ashraf, pointing a gun at him.

'Come on in,' Ashraf said. 'The Scorpion has been expecting you.'

As Aryaman entered the room, Ashraf kicked the door shut. Their guns were pointed at each other.

'Welcome, Aryaman.' A tall, imposing figure walked towards him. He seemed surprisingly young. And his face—not one you would've associated with someone who ran a shadow organization. He looked more like a desk agent.

There was something familiar about his eyes. The rest of his face looked like it had been worked upon, by time. His wiry hair was cropped close to his skull, and his smile revealed everything Aryaman needed to know about the man.

'Remember me?' the Scorpion asked, still grinning.

'Ab-Abhay?' Aryaman stared in disbelief, his gun still pointed at Ashraf.

'It's good to see you again, Aryaman Uncle.'

Aryaman's hands were trembling. To think that Abhay, Amarjyot's son, was the Scorpion!

'Your father . . .'

'Is dead, thanks to you,' Abhay said flatly. 'You and your band of idiots. The Phoenix 5. Dad always had an affinity for these fancy codenames. Wonder what he thinks of the Scorpion.'

'You killed my wife,' Aryaman said. 'You killed Randheer.'

Abhay shook his head. 'She was getting in our way. Funny that it had to be her of all people. But well, you took someone I loved, and I did the same. So we are even.'

'I loved your father like I would my own,' Aryaman said through gritted teeth. 'The mission failed because of all of us. Not him or me alone.'

Ashraf listened to them in rapt attention, joining the dots wherever he could.

'You didn't have to do this, Abhay.'

'Do you even know what happened to my mother after my father's death? Her immune system broke down. She stopped eating and shrivelled to the bone. Cancer consumed her. We did not have enough money to treat her either. And there was nobody to go to. The pension was dismal. She withered away before my eyes. A patriot's wife had no money to fight a disease. That is how the country treated us after all my father had given to it.'

Aryaman was silent.

'Which is why I did what I did, Aryaman. I put all these high-level operatives and mercenaries together to drive an ideology that doesn't require one to only think of their country. But to put themselves before everything else. Their needs—money or otherwise—will be fulfilled as we change the map of South Asia one step at a time. And then, we can go to a higher level with a bigger network of spies—including those who are still serving and those who have gone rogue.'

'If your father were to see you like this, it would have killed him,' Aryaman said. 'You have worked against his principles, against the kind of person he was.'

'That's the point,' Abhay said, exasperated. 'You have given everything to the country. You, my father, Randheer, the others. And what did you get in return? Jail? Death? Was any of it worth it?'

Abhay indicated Ashraf to lower his gun. Ashraf obeyed and stepped backwards. There was an open laptop on the table.

'Join us, Aryaman.'

Aryaman lowered his weapon too. He looked at his feet. His mind had gone numb.

'Join me,' Abhay said. 'We can take over the world if we join forces. Enough of doing the right thing for the country. Do the right thing for yourself. Our first attack in India was a success. You are a lone wolf to them. Their intelligence services abandoned you long ago.'

After a few moments of silence, Aryaman looked Abhay right in the eye. 'Your attack in India was a failure,' he said.

Ashraf jumped into the conversation. 'That's ridiculous. You did it in front of all of us.'

Aryaman shook his head. 'There are some people money can't buy. Their love for the country exceeds everything else. The gas that we let out was a decoy.'

Abhay threw Ashraf a scathing look. 'But . . . The news? The antidote camps? The quarantine?'

'It was all part of the plan.' Aryaman smiled. 'We led you to believe that it worked. I was the only Indian infected by it. And, I've survived.'

Ashraf's face went white. Abhay's nostrils had begun to flare, and his eyes grew fierce. He pulled out his pistol and, with a clean shot, killed Ashraf. The blood splattered over the walls and furniture. Aryaman watched the body drop to the ground; he watched the sea of blood spilling out.

'Abhay,' Aryaman said. 'It's over. Turn yourself in and start afresh.' Pointing his gun at Abhay, Aryaman stepped towards him.

'You mean like you did?' Abhay laughed nervously. 'No thanks.' He had his gun trained at Aryaman.

'I don't want to be the one taking your life,' Aryaman said. 'For whatever it's worth, you are Amarjyot's son.'

'I'm going to shoot you and get the fuck out of here.'

'That's not possible,' Aryaman said. 'Our agents have secured the building by now. There's no escape. Turn yourself in.'

'The network that I have begun,' Abhay said with some confidence, 'is way bigger than you can imagine. The attack in Mumbai may have failed, but what I have planned goes beyond that. Arresting me won't mean I will stop what has been set in motion. You will spend the rest of your life trying to figure out a way to stop what I have started.'

'If you stop that,' Aryaman said, 'you have a shot at a normal life.'

'Normal life?' Abhay smiled despondently. 'It's too late for that, isn't it?'

His finger was firm on the trigger. Aryaman was expecting the bullet, and he dived for cover.

But Abhay had put the gun to his own throat.

'I'll die like my father. Except on my own terms.'

'No!' Aryaman leapt forward to stop him.

But Abhay had pulled the trigger, and that was that.

Dehradun, a month later . . .

Aryaman was beginning to like his new lifestyle. The greenery around him; the jovial kids strumming guitars; his son coming out to play after finishing homework; Avantika reading books in the library; his mother and him sitting silently, doing nothing; Chor settling in their laps. He wanted the rest of his life to be this way. And it seemed like it was going to, until Bipin Sharma decided to drop in uninvited one day, ruining the dinner plans Aarti had made for that evening.

Sharma lit a cigarette and when he offered one to Aryaman, he took it almost instantly.

'I thought you didn't smoke?' Sharma said with a wry smile.

'Why are you here?' Aryaman asked bluntly.

Sharma handed Aryaman an iPad. Aryaman swiped through some documents on it, smoking away all the while, his eyebrows furrowed in concentration. He then slid the iPad back to Sharma.

'So?' Aryaman asked.

'At least five attacks in motion, Aryaman. We believe there is more to this than meets the eye. Abhay might have been led into this by higher forces that made him the Scorpion. And the people doing this don't know that the Scorpion is dead. If we impersonate the Scorpion smartly enough, we can figure the details out and bring them down.'

'We?' Aryaman scoffed. 'There is no "we".'

'It's fairly simple,' Sharma said. 'You step into the Scorpion's shoes and unearth the various attacks that he has planned. You can do it from the confines of your home and you will have our entire machinery at your disposal.'

Chor came running towards Aryaman and leapt into his lap.

'Chor,' Aryaman said, rubbing the dog's belly. 'Uncle here wants me to leave you again. No? I shouldn't? Okay. I won't.'

Aryaman turned to Sharma. 'You hear that, uncle?'

Sharma smiled and stood up. He left the iPad behind for Aryaman.

'In case you change your mind,' Sharma said. 'Everything you need to begin the mission is in there. It would help us to have you on board.'

Aryaman looked at the iPad as he stroked Chor's head.

'Hope to hear from you,' Sharma said, preparing to leave.

'I wouldn't hold my breath,' Aryaman said with a smile. He then turned to see Avantika and Aarti speaking to each other in the kitchen. 'I have too much to lose if I do this. And God knows I've lost enough.'

Sharma nodded and began to walk away. He then stopped and turned to Aryaman. 'I'm sorry for everything,' he said. 'And thank you for all that you have done.'

Aryaman smiled as he watched Sharma leave. Then, he turned his attention to Chor. But his eyes kept returning to the iPad.